THE OPPORTUNE MOMENT, 1855

OTHER WORKS BY PATRIK OUŘEDNÍK IN ENGLISH TRANSLATION

Europeana: A Brief History of the Twentieth Century
Case Closed

THE OPPORTUNE
MOMENT, 1855
A NOVEL BY
PATRIK OUŘEDNÍK

TRANSLATED BY ALEX ZUCKER

DALKEY ARCHIVE PRESS
CHAMPAIGN AND LONDON

Originally published in Czech as *Příhodná chvíle, 1855* by Torst, 2006
Copyright © 2006 by Patrik Ouředník
Translation copyright © 2011 by Alex Zucker
First edition, 2011

Library of Congress Cataloging-in-Publication Data

Ouredník, Patrik.
[Prihodná chvíle. English]
The opportune moment, 1855 / by Patrik Ouredník ; translated by Alex Zucker. -- 1st ed.
  p. cm.
Originally published: Príhodná chvíle, Prague : Torst, 2006.
ISBN 978-1-56478-596-1 (pbk. : alk. paper)
I. Zucker, Alex. II. Title.
PG5039.25.U74P7513 2011
891.8'635--dc22

                    2010046387

Partially funded by the University of Illinois at Urbana-Champaign and by a grant from the
Illinois Arts Council, a state agency

This translation was subsidized by the Ministry of Culture of the Czech Republic

www.dalkeyarchive.com

Cover: design and composition by Danielle Dutton, illustration by Nicholas Motte
Printed on permanent/durable acid-free paper and bound in the United States of America

MARCH 1902

I

Madam, however strong my distaste at the thought of deferring to your whim after so many years, I have not found within myself the courage to resist it, and am left with no choice but to submit, albeit I do so at the expense of my repute. To oblige you means to confess to my love for you, that transient conflagration, that involuntary clouding of the senses, which renders less persuasive all that I have professed and proclaimed; and as much as you know it, in your selfishness you ask of me a sincerity which I could not show anyone else. For if in life I have resisted your God and his depraved demands, if I have resisted unfreedom and shallowness, if I have faced ridicule and human baseness always with calm and determination—I have lost my struggle with love; and what is more, my love has been embodied by you, a woman unworthy of true emotion. Still today, when I find in you nothing which would be worth attention, when I marvel at the fact that I ever could have loved you, still today a word from your mouth knocks me defenseless to my knees, returning me to the days of immaturity and youthful fumbling, to days past and past perfect, to the juvenile schoolboy who carried out directions and instructions he did not understand. But the schoolboy in the end revolted and made up his mind to submit only to that which appeared sensible and good to him, whereas the aging man takes pen in hand and hastens to satisfy your vanity.

You wish for me to "describe the novel of my life"—so long since we have seen each other! But my life, Madam, is no novel which you could have bound between covers and deposited in the library at the mercy of mold and your friends' wrinkled fingers. My life is my work, which in spite of scorn and ridicule I have built in faraway Brazil; my life and my work are one and the same. My work, however artless, however fragile and unfinished, has been useful; my life has thus not been in vain.

Novel! The pages which I have decided in this way to make public are not, Madam, a recounting of actuality, but the memoirs of a stranger. You will soon comprehend why I speak of a stranger; but first, if you please, let us be clear what we mean when we say memoir, which the theory of literature so foolishly converts into the plural, as if one *memoir* were not enough, as if memory were but the murmur of a reed shaken in the wind, and by multiplying the murmurs something of note would result. I do not, Madam, have any intention of yielding to the canons of contemporary literature, which ask authors to make entertaining monstrosities of their private lives; nor do I intend to submit to those who style themselves literary critics, those Benedictines of vanity and slippery surface, who in books seek only sentences which enable them to emasculate the truth, to stifle light under the fashionable cover of modern psychology and literary science.

To be sure, trapped in snares, man grasps for compromise and libation. I am no more resistant than others: I too might have gravitated toward portraying some of the scenes which have shaken my conscience, as writers tend to do when they wish to draw attention to a thing which seems important to them to describe. They give form to their stories so as to *inform* about the thing; already the ancient Greeks believed that only in this way was it possible to reach man in the thinking realms of his soul. It is a cheap and embarrassing fraud—for what reason does one hearken more attentively to the artfully written than the unartfully spoken?—but it is what people, lamentably, demand; and the people of your world doubly so. So I too, in the vain belief that it would do my tale some good, might sooner or later have taken recourse to those ridiculous dodges on which readers in their folly so insist—to direct and indirect speech (how odd, to talk in *indirect* speech!), to allegories and hyperboles, intrigues and anecdotes, irony and persiflage, the anaphors and litotes in which you were so skilled. I might have taken recourse to all these trivialities in the name of my former love for you; and because it is what people, lamentably, demand. Fate and chance, however, have decided to save me from that; and should I perpetrate such dodges in this letter, which constitutes the introduction to my own story, be aware that it is unintentional.

My work is my life; but since life lasts years, while work only an instant, I shall attempt to specify the paths by which my thinking has proceeded. Then I shall leave the word to another.

I do not shun writing—merely literature. In writing is truth; in literature, lies. He who writes, probes his loins and finds words; he who writes literature, stacks them in heaps. Literature is a way to avoid facing writing, to declare a lie with impunity. Nothing terrifies writers of literature more than writing; and, wishing to escape it, they seek refuge in literature which weaves entanglements and entangles itself in foolish affairs. Words are to them as indifferent as bricks to the mason, characters are for them mere empty vessels into which they pour false passions and untrue emotions.

For only he who has lived his life can breathe it into words. I have lived through this and that and discovered the meaning of my existence. I also discovered its limits; limits, however, are flexible, whereas meaning is eternal.

Never, Madam, have I longed to be a writer, to be one of those who substitute words for deeds, who take recourse in the world of rhetoric so as to conceal their cowardice, too weak and impotent to face it with open visor, too hypocritical to admit to it, even if but fleetingly, if only inadvertently. Words! My love for you was boundless; remember that September day when I told you—with trembling voice, tears in my eyes—My love for you, Julia, is boundless. How much stronger would my love have been had I recited my confession in Alexandrines instead of in a few simple words? What a shallow creature is man! No, my love could not have been stronger; and had your reply been otherwise, I would have died of happiness on the spot. But it is likely and tragic that my love might have seemed stronger to you had I arrayed it in verse and—how monstrous a word!—*informed* you of it thus. Words, words, words! In the depths of night sometimes I plunge into a mad dream: that one day people will do without words and speak with one another using nothing but the gaze of their eyes in infinite love and kindness, in the mutual understanding of free beings.

II

I was born the day the Spanish revolt was suppressed in the bloody storming of Trocadéro. My mother was in the service of a Genovese attorney who got her with child. After she had given birth, he sent her back to Pisa, where she had come from, with a promise to provide for his illegitimate child. And he kept his promise: My mother regularly received money from him for my upbringing and studies. Even later, however, he did not express any desire to meet me.

I have never concealed my bastard origin; on the contrary, I find in it further evidence of how ridiculous it is to divide people into classes—and how ridiculous are those who dream of installing a classless society by diktat, in the foolish belief that it is enough to declare a law for people to renounce the feeling of social exclusivity. Even at the cost of a million lives, one cannot hope to stop the vain aristocrat from filing his nails and admiring himself in the mirror; the upstart twit from setting stock in the twittishness to which he owes his wealth; the semi-literate scholar from holding up his semi-literate martinetism as a thing to be admired. Remake the world? Did we learn nothing from the French Revolution? There is only one way to create not an egalitarian but a *fraternal* society, and that is to join forces with those who think the same way and *voluntarily* build a new world, far away from the old one, a world without a past, without hatred, and then—perhaps!—sheerly by virtue of its existence, its peace-loving nature, and its dignity, it will, step by step, influence others to think the same. Perhaps that is what the Quakers were dreaming of when they set out for the New World. But their aspiration was futile from the outset because they brought with them their own God, a God even more merciless than the one their fathers had worshiped. Their aspiration was futile from the outset because their aspiration was to live freely in slavery. And in the slavery of the mind to which they so stubbornly clung, they murdered the natives and had slaves of the body shipped in from distant lands. The number of slaves you have reflects the number of times that God has looked upon you with pleasure—that was their *credo*.

After studies in Pisa and Perugia, I received my degree as a healer and veterinarian, and moved to Genoa. There, as you know, I enrolled in a course of philosophical studies, which I finished in Lyons. Four years later, fate blew me to Geneva, and a year after that to Vienna, where I met you. Of the year and a half I spent there, you know as much as I. From Vienna I went first to Tunis with the vague intention of forgetting Europe, but the dismal living conditions there forced my early return to Italy. I settled down in Cuneo and opened a veterinary practice. The following months, I admit, I suffered in agony; your decision seared me like a red-hot iron. Why were we not able to find a way to each other, despite my willingness—and, dare I say, your inclination toward me? What was it that kept us apart? What is it that makes a person so obstinate, so aloof? Why is it that people are not closer to one another? Why are the natural aspirations of humans so often frustrated by the rules and automatic behaviors to which we accede like unresisting puppets, filled with sawdust and slavishly submissive? Why is it that people are not able to listen to one another, that every conversation is nothing but the affectation of opinion, the result of mindless, ingrained reflexes which have absolutely nothing in common with either reason or emotion? I speak here not of social conventions, which are in and of themselves unimportant, but of people's scant longing for liberty. Why is it that people are so afraid of freedom?

Ah! Why write about freedom to someone who has lived only for herself? You lack neither feeling nor intelligence, of that I have had the possibility to persuade myself many times. But of what use to you is feeling and intelligence? Often we have spoken together of the *century of light*, what the French call *les Lumières*, the Germans *die Aufklärung*, the English *the Enlightenment*. Voltaire, Diderot, Rousseau . . . The first enchanted you, the second disturbed you, the third moved you. But! You, Madam, should have wanted the *Encyclopédie* in your library and the Penal Code in the public reading room, bread for all, but a ball gown only for yourself, free love in books, but a husband in life. You profess a dignfied life, but you fear death.

Philosophy? *La belle affaire!* Those whom today we call the light of humanity were perhaps flares rather than torches; we can become them only individually and only so long as we are willing to live our truth in spite of the idols to which the dull crowd, which we call society, kowtows.

Can human truth be concealed in books? Essays! Tracts! Treatises! *Libido sciendi*, you say; to which I reply to you: *Libido dom-*

inandi. Writing books is but another way to enslave one's fellow man, to force one's will on him, to outwit one's smallness and pettiness, to postpone the last sleepless night before death. Even the last of the botanists, occupying himself with the mystery of nature, sooner or later begins to see himself as an expert of the universe with the conviction that he has grasped something, and that something he shall call order; and he shall force his order on the entire world. *Doxa*, Madam, leads his steps, not *epistémé*. In the works of philosophers and scientists alike, we find each time the same thing, the desire to rob the reader of his free will in the name of this or that idol, of the freedom of the human interior in the name of the freedom of the more supreme and orderly. No, Madam, although I concede that in books I have found ideas, incentives, embryos of my later opinions, never in them have I found a recipe for happiness. Science and philosophy cannot lead to freedom. Freedom is the fruit of passion, not of reason; passion is a gift of nature, not of civilization. Freedom springs from our innocence, which science has taken from us.

For two and a half thousand years scholars have perfected their theories, seeking for ever more knowledge, promising a better world—and the world is ever more incomprehensible and painful. Why? The answer is so simple, we refuse to accept it: because they've never rid themselves of their prejudices, because they recognize only that which enters into their "natural order," which they inherit from generation to generation. Certainly this order may allow an exception, a deviation, an anomaly, but to allow the slightest disturbance of the "natural character" of things is out of the question. Ah! What is natural about the fact that man starves, murders, sponges from the misfortunes of others, mates only with the consent of the community, submits to idols? Yes, man is starving and murdering, they say; let us enact a reform that he starve only should it have a higher meaning, and murder solely when it contributes to the Ideal. Let us enact that he may divorce and remarry—what freedom!—that he may choose between this or that idol—what progress! Look around you: as if the growth of human hatred were proportional to the number of proposed reforms. Wars, poverty, confusion, and despair. It is necessary, say the political philosophers, for us to reorganize the state, the church, the administration, the trades, science. Let us reorganize! And let us hide from ourselves the fact that two and a half millennia of reform have brought nothing—and that it is high time we replaced reorganization with *disorganization.* Even without the study of political philosophy you may come to this realization; just suppress the prejudices within yourself. You ask, what does disorganization mean? I reply: to open new paths to human passions. Let us awaken in people an aversion to life in marriage, in domestication, in the city, in civilization; and they will feel a vertiginous bliss at the fact that they may dwell freely with their loved ones anywhere on earth where the soil will feed them. Freedom will replace enslavement, solidarity will replace murdering, envy, and hatred. Is freedom any less passionate than death?

Humanity has succeeded in learning nothing more from history. *Et pour cause*: the revolts against society that have taken place in history have been led in the name of God—a different one, better, purer, more reliable. Man has been sacrificed on his bloody altar. Peasant uprisings? To be sure, hunger drives wolves from the woods. Toss them a bite to eat and they will lick your hand.

The French Revolution? Which one? The one which gave birth to the Declaration on the Rights of Man and of the Citizen? No, I cannot identify even with that. Sovereign nation! Inviolable and *sacred* ownership! Rights one, two, three. Rights! By what right does anyone mean to grant me rights?

Man is born free, but everywhere he is in chains, says Rousseau. To be sure. And what next? The enthronement of a new *order*, the tyranny of the mob. Bloodthirsty fools who grasp hold of any excuse because they lack any reason; cutthroats who claim they intend to dispatch the enemies of the people, and murder the best of their ranks; thieves who plunder public property in the name of the national estates; firebrands who talk of home defense and devastate the land. The only ones of that time who were not hypocrites were the drunkards: they declared that they were thirsty and tapped every keg in sight. Let us respect the drunkards for their forthrightness and arm ourselves against the murderers whose slogan is revolution. Let us respect the drunkards for their unsteady step; he who staggers, murders not.

What else have the reforms brought us? Compulsory school attendance? To what end? So the mob can appropriate the philosophy of the bourgeoisie? Love of property, respect for order, and hatred for everything that transcends them, for everything more true and real? Since when did education ever make a man more human? Better, more perceptive, more insightful? Is not the worst ignorance woven from nonsensical shreds of knowledge filtered by this or that institution, church, state, revolution, monarchy, timocracy, democracy? Compulsory school attendance is the best way there is to multiply the ranks of fools. Do not force anyone to go to school; either he will enroll himself or he will do without it. Do not give people compulsory rights. Do not give them rights or obligations. Give them freedom.

Why should I sacrifice to the idols of my time, my generation, my nation? I sacrifice only to one god: my own. You ask, how can I distinguish it from the idols? Quite simply: idols are the work of society, my god was chosen by my conscience. My god does not assign me any obligations other than to sleep, to wake, to work, to eat, to drink, to excrete, to love, to think. To the idols one must sacrifice one's conscience and one's will. You will recognize them easily, they declare as a virtue the most wretched quality of which a human being is capable: obedience. And it doesn't end with that! The sacrifice of your life is not enough for them; they want you to sacrifice the lives of others as well. Here in the name of a bloodthirsty god, there for the honor of the king, today on the altar of homeland, tomorrow in the name of race or civilization. Idols change names the way you change slippers: yesterday one was called Prussia, today it is named Germany; yesterday it required the death of a Bavarian, today it requires the death of a Frenchman. Sometimes it is called Nation, at other times Reason or the Will of the People. The idols have tens and hundreds of names; the most honest of them is *What would the neighbors say?* They have tens and hundreds of names, however only one desire: to beat you down, to destroy you, to dispatch you, to bring you to naught, to turn you into *nothing.*

III

At that time I also began to contribute regularly to anarchist newspapers—*Protest* and *The Atheist*—and issued my first proclamation. It ended with the words: "Once we establish our free settlement, we will be able to say that anarchy is neither a just nor an unjust idea, but simply a fact." Yes, I was in a hurry to put my ideas into practice, to give form to a word which only recently appeared: *socialism*. Not as it is pursued today by communists, but as a reflection of the origin of the word—socius, partner, comrade, friend, *companion*, with whom *together* I face fate. Anarchy in interpersonal relations, love as the expression of a *fait social*, the abolishment of hierarchy, the denial of God, freedom for all, a common lot—that is socialism. How simple, how innovative! Simple, for we need only free ourselves of our habits and prejudices; innovative, for everything begins anew. To people who say, I wish I could start my life over again, yet not lose my memory of the past, I reply: Become anarchists!

Yes, I was in a hurry to put my ideas into practice. Only the reality of things can persuade those who despite their awareness of the malignancy of the society in which they live are not capable of conceding that another world is possible. I was in a hurry to realize at the expense of propaganda; thus it happened that the people who left for Brazil did not have a clear idea of the project. Many of them, as was gradually revealed, had not even read my articles, or had interpreted them in the light of the political lines of the newspapers which had reprinted them without my knowledge. Filled with clairvoyant disgust at society, I had overestimated those in it; I did not imagine that people who all their lives long had been abused and besotted by society could fail to feel the same deep revulsion. At one point I had had a regular column on cases illustrating the tragic impact of the rules to which society submitted: the suicide of lovers whose surroundings denied them free choice, the murder of a vagrant whom the estate owner believed to be a thief, the strangling of a terrified woman by an officer who feared that her weeping would wake the inhabitants of an enemy village, the violation of a young lady for maintaining a relationship with an enemy soldier—in the nineteenth century!—children sold by their own parents, robbery, rape, and torture in wars and insurrections, corrupt courts, financial frauds, political hypocrisy. I had assumed it would be enough to point out the mechanisms of evil, and underestimated the slowness with which people—especially women—shed their prejudices. Yes, Madam, the greatest enemy of everything new is woman, bound by the mental chains of matrimony or whatever other trap in which she seeks the feeling of safety, protection from the uncertainty of centuries and millennia of belittling existence.

This is also why the first and most important rule to which we must accede if we wish to overturn the order of things is the freedom of women. Woman's standing in society is the most monstrous demonstration of men's smallness and foolishness—and women's as well. Man scorns woman deeply, and the acts of courtesy which he shows her are the expression of a hypocrisy which has as its goal to conceal the slavery in which he keeps her. The ideal woman? Bon mots and tittering turns of conversation, to cover up her dullness and intellectual impotence, embroidering family initials on handkerchiefs and singing at the piano, because after all even she has the right to amusement—why, from time to time, even a dog is allowed to bark with no apparent reason. Once or twice a week we may take her out in the streets; and there, in the anonymity of the crowd, let her go ahead and parade her canary-like incomparability, let her shimmy and shake, our flunky, our prettified lackey, a savage whom we keep for our amusement. Her clothing is the denial of common sense, fashion makes of her a primitive social creature from a colonial exhibition: feathers on her head, golden amulet around her neck, face sprinkled with magic powder, painted lashes, earlobes laden with metal hoops, feet misshapen by ritual footwear, pores cloyed with the most ill-sorted oils and scents. And in all this she takes pride: in the brains of slaves vanity is the manifestation of social existence.

And I speak only of Europe! Look at other worlds, look at Africans, look at American Mormons, look at Muslims! A man has several wives, but a woman only one husband. Polygyny yes, polyandry no. A father has the legal right to kill his daughter if she displeases him, but not his son; he may kill his sister if she displeases him. Infidelity is punished by stoning, as custom demands. Walk through the streets of Tunisia! A woman in public may not expose so much as a centimeter of her body, not a single hair, not a single flash of the eyes. Veiled from head to toe she hurries through life like a disgrace to the human race which must be buried while still alive. Streets full of walking mummies! A veil and several layers of fabric protect her from rotting, and still she must cook and bear children for her man. And in all this she takes pride: in the brains of corpses mummification is the ultimate form of visibility. And in all this her man takes strength and delight: the more dead my woman, the greater my god!

I do not demand the *equality* of women; I am talking about freedom. Equality is nothing but another reorganization of the society of men, a new reform: let us allow women to be like us, let us allow them to be murderers, strategists, politicians, irresponsible and selfish beings longing for power. Tell a woman that she may kill, press a rifle into her hand—and she will become as bloodthirsty and contemptible a creature as man. Equality for women? Our erstwhile canary becomes a sheep. She ceases to warble and begins to bleat; then will we be closer in our dullness and unfreedom. This is what is called for today by those who subscribe to the new doctrine, the new idol, which they call feminism.

No—let us not give women equality, let us allow them freedom. The day when woman becomes free will be the dawn of a revolution whose consequences we can hardly imagine. Free woman means the end of religion, of which in her nonfreedom she has been the most fervid supporter. Free woman means the end of wars which mow down men. Free woman means the end of a society in which the strong oppress the weak, the end of prostitution, physical or moral, the end of violence. Free woman is the harbinger of a new humanity, the first step toward the triumph of humanity over man.

The wish is father to the thought? Perhaps. I admit that I have never been a good prophet. But as long as woman is *different* from man, my hope persists. Man has fizzled at everything he has ever undertaken; let us give a chance to woman.

And before all else: let us abolish marriage! Freed of its tyranny—pedantic or condescending, cruel or feeble, indifferent or loving—woman will acquire consciousness of herself. Marriage! Rousseau is right a hundred times over! If I could rid humanity of a single plague (locusts, religion, cholera, pestilence, private property, wars, government, parliaments, or national revivalists), I would choose marriage—font of unfreedom, hypocrisy, and stupidity.

IV

Free man is dangerous. At least so believe the police, the courts, and the lackeys of society. I have been followed and spied on. Who am I? Where did I come from? Where am I going? Why? What do I write? Why? The first search of my home produced nothing: a few manuscripts of unfinished articles. But have I called in my articles for the overthrow of the government? Not at all, Your Graciousness, I am against all forms of violence. The second search was more thorough: a scalpel was discovered in my veterinary bag. What's this? You are against all forms of violence and you secrete weapons in your apartment? Three months' imprisonment and a liberating verdict with qualification: henceforth I am required to report to the police any and all journeys beyond the city borders. My guardian angels go round to the local farmers and breeders: if we were you, we would entrust our animals to more qualified hands. You never know what to expect from an anarchist. I am practically without work, money is dwindling.

I have been accused of rabble-rousing, subversion of the state—but also of reactionism and conservatism! As gradually there was more and more talk about the Fraternitas settlement, the attacks in the press increased, from irony and bourgeois sarcasm in the pro-government dailies to charges of cowardice and fatalism on the part of self-styled revolutionaries. "When the throat of the proletariat is gripped by hunger, when revolution is a matter of life and death, those who leave on the eve of the battle are cowards and deserters." I have never responded to such attacks: why try to explain that if I belong to no army and I am my own commander, then to speak of desertion is meaningless? Let the communists sacrifice themselves on the altar of the proletariat, if they believe that they will liberate man by doing so; I shall try to liberate man without regard for the proletariat. The working class is but one more idol, the proletariat merely a crippled progeny whose forebears are called hatred, vengefulness, and lack of imagination, the spore of bourgeois thinking, from which they allegedly seek to be emancipated. Program? The dictatorship of some to the detriment of others. The communists are simply continuing the work of the puritans: *Proletarians of all countries, unite*, workers against bourgeoisie, conscious against unconscious, believers against unbelievers, healthy against sickly, obedient against disobedient. Along with the nationalists and the puritans, the communists are the fiercest enemies of the human race and the greatest threat of the new century; I thank nature that I will not be in it long. Mark my words: sooner or later they will all begin to exterminate one another, for they have the same goal, to destroy man in the name of the *organization* of humanity, in the name of a new *arrangement*, in the name of a final *order*. Babeuf! Blanqui! Once upon a time hatred for man was a reflection of hatred for humanity. Today we are more progressive: there has been born a new hatred, a hatred out of *love* for humanity. The happiness of man is not a right but a requirement—the communists teach us that. You do not want to be happy with us? Die! Serve God, serve the nation, serve humanity, the desire of all who are inferior is *to serve*—anything but freedom. A free man is inscrutable; he might refuse our services. You do not want me to serve you? Die!

I know that even among anarchists there are today many who perceive hatred as the reflection of a more lively, just, and generous love of life, who believe that there can be no love of freedom without hatred of those who rob us of it. I have never shared this view: the freedom of society leads through the freedom of the individual; I do not believe that man can attain freedom at the cost of killing, even if it is a matter of doing away with tyrants.

If someone should want to murder me, I shall defend myself. First I shall attempt to dispose of him without greater violence; but should he be stronger than I, I shall attempt to kill him. My life as a peace-loving man is more valuable than the life of a murderer. Individual defense is permissible, as it corresponds to the laws of nature. However, defense through aggression in the name of "higher interests" submits to the same logic as war, returning us to the civilization we seek to overcome. Hence I have always been against anarchistic violence, whatever form it may take: violence and war are one and the same.

Yes, I deny the necessity of any form of war, both aggressive and so-called defensive, or, as they say nowadays, patriotic. A free man has no *patrie*. A free man, apart from his freedom, has nothing of *his own*. My pacifism has nothing in common with God and with all those who appeal to *Thou shalt not kill*. I do not believe in a higher order which would forbid me to kill. And if I did think God existed, I would have to come to the conclusion that he wants war—because it goes on. Which would give me sufficient reason to damn him, instead of bowing to him. And due to my peace-loving nature—forgive me this cheap irony—I would end up in hell. But the injunction of respect for one's neighbor is human, not divine. And should we forget respect, there remains common sense. Wars waged "for rational reasons" are either the greatest hypocrisy or the ultimate idiocy. Were people to have a little more rationality in them, war today would be a forgotten word.

V

The attacks in the press at least had the advantage that they also spread information about my project. People, it seems, do not have great trust in journalists: in spite of the criticism and ridicule, the project began to attract many more people than I had originally anticipated. In Piemont, Tuscany, Liguri, Lombardi, and Savoy in France, there suddenly sprang up groups of activists who organized lectures, charitable markets, and raffles. The oddest assortment of objects began coming in to the editor's office: tawdry trinkets, books, quilts, clocks, hunting arms, armchairs, pictures; someone arrived in a wagon loaded with boards and netting; countryfolk sent hens, hares, geese, pigs, goats. For the most part they were people who had no intention of leaving; they wanted merely to express their sympathies and help the settlers.

But the number of true prospects was increasing also, and not only among workers and craftsmen. Among the candidates were an Austrian officer, an agricultural engineer, a Siennese pharmacist, scions of the finest families in France were applying . . . but also pimps offering "women accustomed to men in great quantities" (!). In the first year, while I was still considering an appropriate place to establish the settlement, I received more than four hundred applications, roughly a quarter of which came from married couples or families with children: all told, nearly seven hundred settlers! The Society for the Establishment and Development of the Fraternitas Free Settlement was created in Lyons, followed by the Society for a New Life, which eventually took over all the bookkeeping; the Society for Free Socialism was created in Genoa, and branches of an association called Far From the Capital in Le Havre and Paris.

Where was I to locate my experimental settlement? Experiments such as this were doomed to failure in Europe; the pressure of the surroundings was too great, too present, communication with the outside world too easy and seductive. Canada was a land of hunters, farmland was expensive. In the United States there was no place for a free-thinking group of people: the land belonged in equal parts to Pistol Petes and Puritans, who shared the same fetish: *In God we trust.* I considered French Polynesia for a time, but the conditions there were too harsh. Then I concentrated on Central and South America, Mexico, Venezuela, and finally Brazil. The climate and agricultural potential were not ideal, but at least they were decent. The Brazilian government was favorable toward immigration and made us a very advantageous offer: exemption from taxes and customs fees for three years, plus an interest-free loan payable over six years, in return for a commitment of at least 5,000 permanent settlers on the territory provided during that time.

I set out for Brazil that same year. I arrived on the site of the future settlement during the rains, but despite the inclement weather I was enchanted. For the first time in years the image of your face in my memory began to dissolve. For the first time in years I felt free once again. Suddenly I was seized by the awareness that a solution was within reach. Had the civilized world ever been closer to extinction than now? European civilization! Paris and its extravagant sophisticates, Vienna and its diligent informers, London and its Salvation Army brass bands, Amsterdam and its pudgy gold dealers, Rome and its papists! Was it not the opportune moment to quit this world burdened with misfortune and misery, caked in oozing ulcers, pallid and exhausted, and show it that the path it has been following thus far is only one of many possible? Or is there only one world possible and will people be forever slaves, no matter what we call them? What does your *Encyclopédie* have to say to that?

VI

Last night I had a dream about you. I was myself—an old man— you were still young. So beautiful! So foreign!

All our ideas about death are childish. Some believe that man does not die; others, that death is nothing, for if we do not live, death does not exist. But, on the contrary, that answers nothing, if death exists only in life, it means merely that life is mortal, death immortal. Death, in its immortality, is ironic, more ironic than life itself.

Take for instance a mother's first act after giving birth: quieting the child's anxiety, lightening the burden for the life she has just brought into the world. A newborn cries through his first weeks and months of life. How come? In anticipation of what awaits him? A clairvoyance, which he will later lose, at the instant we force on him the illusion we ourselves have lost, the illusion of safety, the illusion of eternity? Which he will lose until the moment he reaches maturity and sees through it, definitively and irrevocably?

The parents' role? To encourage their child to live, to ease his fear, to soothe him, calm him, arrange the home for him along the pattern of intestines, arouse in him the idea that he is still in the safety of the womb, persuade him that the surrounding world is only scenery, a stage set at which we gaze peacefully from our hiding place in the darkness of the audience. Any parent who prematurely reveals to his child that the human theater is played once and for all, that no one will mend the ragged costumes, and that the blood flowing from the boards is real, will be morally condemned by other parents: How could he be so *inhuman*? The parents' secrets protect the child—and excuse the parents.

I lay in bed in an unknown room, imbrued with sweat; you were holding my hand and smiling. I felt no desire, just joy and peace. One thing alone clouded my happiness, drops of sweat, flowing into my eyes, which forced me to blink and prevented me from seeing you more clearly. Wanting to rid myself of this veil of tears I shook my head, but succeeded only in sending a sharp pain down my spine. The sound of voices came from the next room, men's and women's. They sounded unnatural, quarrelsome and shrill. I realized that we were in a hotel room and the voices were actually coming from the corridor or the lobby. Then you spoke, with a kind smile and tenderness in your eyes, but your voice sounded like the voices of those outside: unnatural, quarrelsome, shrill. You said: Where will we go now?

VII

To justify life! The optimists—those affable, rosy-cheeked, smiling people—believe that everything is in perfect order. All the horrors of the world, all human spite and folly, all that is a natural part of life. How pessimistic! The pessimists on the other hand—those gloomy, petulant, bilious, obstinate individuals—believe that life should be better, that it *could* be something other than spiteful and foolish. How optimistic!

I am aware of the extent of the commitment which I have taken upon myself: people who in good faith set out across the ocean and whose way back is now closed view me rightfully as the co-author of their fate. Yes, I should have expressed myself more circumspectly, paid more attention to recruitment and various instructions which were issued under my moral aegis—many of them, as I have bitterly come to realize over the years, in conflict with my deepest-held convictions. Some fools even published some sort of Regulations under my name—as if anarchy could *regulate* something! Yes, I let myself be carried away by my visions and succumbed to the superficial enthusiasm which dominated after my first proclamations.

However, the short-lasted duration of the settlement is not proof of the project's unattainability—only people without imagination could think so. If the first experiment fails to produce the expected results, it must be repeated. Galileo spent many an evening observing the chandelier in the Pisa Cathedral; why should it be any different with anarchy? Can people live together without laws? Experience has shown that yes: a group of people, including those with no clear concept of anarchy, lived together for nearly three years—and notwithstanding the aforementioned Regulations, with no preordained rules. As long as voluntary labor held up, there was plenty of food and trust alike. And if people began to suffer from hunger, it was not because it was impossible to assure the influx of provisions, but the fault of the self-appointed managers. If the people did not get bread, it was because no one mended the granary roof, damaged by torrential rains. If the livestock trampled the bean fields, it was because the cattle run was shoddily constructed. And if the settlers were overcome with indifference, it was due to lack of faith; some of them lost trust and infected the others, refusing to fetch water or to go and work in the field. The idiotic principles of parliamentarianism squeezed out anarchy. The settlers adopted an absurd system of referenda, squandering time in assemblies which begot nothing but ridiculous promises and individual ambitions. They then dictated to others their *rights* and *obligations* . . . And then—only then!—the diseases we know so well began to creep into the settlement like a plague: restriction of freedom, spying, envy and jealousy, disrespect for women, theft, and, finally, murder.

Yes, I arrived late. The delay on the sea—four and a half months instead of two!—was the final spitefulness of fate; had the ship landed five or six weeks earlier, I might have been able to achieve something yet.

What to add? Never, not even after our breakup, had I felt greater hopelessness. For three days I wandered the deserted settlement, trying to understand. I addressed myself to the police in Curitiba, the farmers from Guaragi and Imbituva, no one knew a thing; I returned to Paranaguá in the hope that I would run into some settlers, in vain. The only thing I mined from my journey was a journal given me by the police officer charged with the investigation. The whole affair had long since ceased to interest him, assuming it ever had. In his eyes the Europeans who came to Brazil were nothing but rogues and beggars, and the *Casa Fraternidade* was further evidence of the fact that Europeans would have done better to conduct their experiments at home and not make extra work for the Brazilian police.

In the end I tarried six years in Brazil; there was no reason to return, nor anywhere to return to—I had lost my practice in Cuneo. I lectured in São Paulo on socialism at first, then set out with a puppet theater across the Rio Grande do Sul. I lectured six months at the Agricultural School in Porto Alegre, and for three years ran the agronomic center in Bahia. Some longtime friends tracked me down there and persuaded me to return to Italy to help them run a Collective Agricultural and Industrial Cooperative in Lombardy. It exists to this day, perhaps it is even prospering.

For several years I attempted to build a new anarchist settlement in Venezuela. However, it quickly became clear that my reputation and name would henceforth be an obstacle to similar projects.

Since then I have eked out a living. Nothing that would interest you.

Oh, yes, I have a son, he lives in Brazil. He, too, longs for a world that is not a prison. Today he, too, has a grown-up son; so he has someone to whom he can pass on his despair. Nothing new under the sun. In our youth we live in expectation of better tomorrows, in old age that time seems to us happier than the tomorrows that never came. We have forgotten how hopeless hope can be, how unbearable the waiting. Disappointment has become commonplace for us. We are accustomed to it. In reality we are better off than our sons.

Well then, Madam, what more could you want from me? Regret? Repentance? A humble return to the human fold?

The world is pure madness. Man is born in chains. Into a world of hatred and evil. Searching his way in the cold toward the rot. Few yearn to become killers, but few refuse to kill. Evil winds through history without end. Wagons along muddied trails. I do not know whether to understand evil makes a man more clairvoyant. I do not know whether it makes him stronger waiting for death. I know only this: I await my own calmly, resigned and without regret.

JANUARY–APRIL 1855

We arrived in Paris four days late because of cholera and compulsory quarantine in Grenoble. 11 of us died in quarantine: 5 men, 1 woman, and 5 children. We divided up their money without regard to age; for their clothes and other things we drew lots. I got a set of sewing needles and a collapsing telescope.

Paris is a big city, bigger than I'd imagined. Cursio was also surprised. He said: I knew it was the capital, with many people living in it, but I didn't expect that many. What insanity!

Old man Agottani and Zeffirino Soldi went to the offices of the Society for a New Life, where they handed in a list of settlers and reserved berths on the ship that's sailing from Le Havre. They brought back a receipt for the settlement supplier and some other documents. Some are in Italian, others in French. As they were coming out of the place, the police stopped them and took down their names.

We visited the market, the Palace of Industry, an island in the center of the city, and a cemetery.

We took the train to Rouen, where we boarded a ship to Le Havre (the railway stops there). The train passed through Pontoise, Alincourt, Hacqueville, Gaillardbois, from Rouen to Le Havre along a river through La Bouille, Jumièges, and Quillebeuf. Decio asked why I was writing down the names of the cities and towns. I explained that I was keeping a journal. He asked why I hadn't kept one in Italy. I explained that at first it hadn't occurred to me, but reading the List of Necessities had given me the idea. Eventually, I said, I would copy the Settlement Regulations and the Settler's Handbook into it, too, and any other documents, and that way I would have a chronicle of the settlement. He asked me where I'd learned to write and whether I'd gone to school. I said the local priest in Brescia had taught me. He said religion keeps people in darkness and priests bamboozle people. He said he didn't want any religion except fraternity and free love. He said, write *that* down. Just wait till the priest sees that, and he laughed.

There's a big port in Le Havre, and a museum with ships in it.

We spent the night at an inn. The next day we visited the port and the museum and bought supplies for the settlers from a list worked out by Zeffirino Soldi: tools and utensils, clothing (long-sleeve shirts, undershirts, underwear, stockings, socks, three pairs of pants, suspenders, work smocks, hooded raincoat, jacket), footwear (two pair of boots), bedding and other personal items, toothbrush, comb, two razors, mirror, towels (2), razor strop or hone (I bought a hone), pocket knife, eating utensils, knives, needles (didn't buy), two dozen spools of white thread (bobbins) and two dozen black, knitting needles, inkwell, ink, quills (6), notebook, penknife, dishes, clogs, watering can, chamber pot, brushes for clothes and boots, beard comb (for men), salve, quinine, steamer trunk (not too bulky). For women Zeffirino also recommends three pair of cotton stockings, 4 white and 2 colored panties, 4 summer and 4 winter skirts, 3 three-corner scarves and a dozen shoulder scarves, two aprons, 1 hairbrush, 1 hair clasp, 1 emery board and 1 nail brush, other toiletries and hygiene supplies at personal discretion, but nothing showy.

The shopping took up our whole afternoon. We left the goods on the pier and took turns standing watch. I watched from 2 in the morning to 4:15. I was cold and couldn't sleep.

We left the inn at quarter to 7 in the morning. The streets were icy and Adelina and Argia fell on the slippery pavement. Decio said: It's as if this nasty weather was trying to tell us there's no need to regret the world we're leaving behind. Giacomo said: I don't regret it! Umberto said: No one does!

The ship is called the *Southern Cross*. We loaded our things into cutters and the sailors rowed us to the ship. Besides us there were also several dozen Frenchmen and some Austrians coming aboard. An argument broke out over when we would sail. Some said the next day with the incoming tide, but Giacomo pointed out that there were almost no sailors on board and lots of supplies still left on the pier, but the cabin boy explained that they belonged to other ships. Others said we were still waiting for the rest of the settlers, and there would be three or four hundred of us, since there were many courageous and skillful people in Europe just waiting for the right opportunity to build a new world. There are fifty-five of us Italians:

Elisabetta Arrighini
Amilcare Beretti
Egizio Cicali
Cursio Corsi
Marco Agottani
Aldino Agottani (brother)
Tranquillo Agottani (father)
Monica Levi
Luisa Torti
Erasmo Torti (brother)
Carlo Torti (brother)
Adelina Artusi

Virginio Artusi (brother)
Aniceto Artusi (father)
Zeffirino Soldi
Vito Ferroni
Lorenzo Cappato
Pietro Varisone
Anna Dolfi
Ezio Ruggera
Argia Fagnoni

(I'll continue the list tomorrow.)

February 1st

There really aren't many sailors on board, and when we asked the captain about it, he explained that a man in Le Havre was supposed to supply a full crew, but the recruiters had come and taken away six sailors whose numbers were drawn in the lottery for the army.

Today the Germans who missed yesterday's boarding rowed up in three big cutters. They clambered up the ropes and one woman fell and split her head on the edge of a cutter. Umberto Verona, who worked at the slaughterhouse in Livorno, examined her, but it was too late. The sailors carried the corpse back to the city with them. One of the German men also wanted to go back, but the rest of them surrounded him and persuaded him not to.

The passage takes about two months. We set sail at a quarter past twelve.

Most of us stayed on board, watching the land fade into the distance until a thin strip was all that was left, but some people got seasick and didn't last till the end. In fact almost everyone.

Achille Gallina
Pietro Riva
Cattina Dondelli
Mario Carosi
Domenico Codega
Pietro Colli
Paolo Costagli
Francesca Reboa
Achille Dondelli
Carla Mezzadri
Primo Crollanti
Domenico Parodi
Livia Dabrigi
Tristana Renzi
Manfredi Renzi
Cecilia Negri
Amos Vallone
Umberto Verona

(I'll continue the list tomorrow.)

February 2nd

Below decks there's almost no lighting at all and vomit everywhere. We're divided into compartments of nine people each. The tickets say "second-class cabin" but they aren't really cabins.

February 4th

Aurelio Gattai
Rina Gattai
Pietro Gavarri
Antonio Massa
Eugenio Grassi
Eugenia Grassi
Carla Gaibi
Decio Boni
Giacomo Zerla
Alessandro Mansueto
Alessandro Mostaca
Giovanni Bossi
Rinaldo Garzino
Adele Servanti
Luigi Silano
Bruno Celli

(The end.)

February 6th

This morning some of the sailors on deck were having an argument and failed to carry out the commands of the first officer quickly enough, so he took a pole from the windlass and began to beat them with it. One he hit so hard that he collapsed to the deck covered in blood. Achille Dondelli, Domenico, and Umberto tried to help the sailor, but the officer drove them back and ordered us to remain in our designated berths.

February 7th

The captain and the first officer are both Americans. The first officer is vicious and cunning, pelting the sailors with whatever comes to hand and kicking them constantly. The shipmaster is Portuguese and speaks a little Italian. The crew is made up of various nationalities and includes three Negroes, whom the officers beat like horses. When they want to speak with the captain, they have to wait by his cabin without knocking until someone else comes along and knocks on his door. The cook is a Negro, too. His name is Samba and his hair is white.

February 9th

The Germans are poorer than us Italians, and most of them have hardly anything of their own. We're worried that they might try to steal some of our things. Zeffirino suggested that we keep watch at night. But Decio disagreed. He said: We're sailing towards a world where everything will be shared, including property and women alike. Zeffirino said that for property to be shared, first there has to be some, and if some scoundrels go and steal ours, the only thing we'll have left to share is s—. And then he said: The women can look out for themselves. Cattina said she wouldn't sleep with a German even if he begged her on his knees. Umberto said he would be happy to sleep with a German, and Cattina said that was just like him. Zeffirino suggested that only those who agreed with him keep watch, and that he would take the first shift. Fifteen people signed up. But Decio said majority rules and we didn't leave the Old World behind so we could make the same mistakes and submit to the decrees of self-styled leaders. Zeffirino said he left to find freedom and wouldn't take orders from anyone. Vito Ferroni said Decio was right, matters affecting everyone should be decided by majority, the settlement regulations said so. Zeffirino said we weren't in the settlement yet, and once we were, the Germans would be there with us, but until then we had to look out for ourselves. Giacomo suggested we go below decks and see whether anything of ours was missing, and if so we keep watch, and if not we trust the Germans. The suggestion was adopted with a majority of thirty-seven votes. Giacomo and Zeffirino went to the first officer to borrow the key to the storeroom, but he said it was out of the question, they might steal something there.

Elisabetta is a year older than me, and after dinner we sit together in a cutter on the starboard side.

There are more than 200 passengers on board, mostly German, French, and Italian. The Germans are poor and filthy, and there are more of them than anyone else. Some of the Germans and the French live together, and Mr. Mangin goes above deck to sleep because he can't stand the filth. There aren't enough sailors, so the captain has hired on eight of the Germans. There are also two Americans on board, and a lady from Vienna with a female companion who chews tobacco, but they aren't settlers. There are some other Austrians also, but it's hard to tell them apart from the Germans, unless they stay in a different part of the ship. There are also a few Austrians who don't speak German but some other language even the captain doesn't understand. And there is one Swiss family with three children who stay in the first-class cabins. The captain speaks French and a little bit of German. Some of the Austrians are settlers, but not all. All of them are against the occupation of Piemont, though. One of the Germans told Agottani that the Austrians who don't speak German speak a dialect from eastern Germany called Slavic. But Decio said it isn't a dialect but the language spoken by Serbs. There's also a Belgian man who's short and fat and his name is

Atlant. All of the food has a salty taste, and we each get 1.5 liters of water a day.

One of the Germans died. The sailors wrapped his body in canvas and tied a sack of rocks to his feet. Then they laid him on a plank, sprinkled him with dirt, and rolled the corpse into the sea. Almost all the men on board removed their hats, but not all. Manfredi had been wondering why we had rocks on board. One of the sailors said: Now you have your answer.

When the weather is nice we dine on deck with the French. After dinner they sing the Marseillaise or other songs. We sing a song that Paolo wrote. The chorus goes: *We're sailing to where they roast coffee, where they roast coffee, where they boast coffee.* Elisabetta has a nice voice.

The *Southern Cross* is a four-master with no steam engine; the masts and bridges are mostly still made of wood. There are two sails on the first mast and one each on the others.

Some of the Germans are so poor that they've begun asking us for the potato peels we've been tossing into the sea.

February 15th

Most of us Italians are anarchists, but most of the French are communists and are constantly calling meetings. They argue among themselves more than us Italians or the Germans and the Austrians, but every time an argument breaks out, five minutes later they're all hugging each other again and singing the Marseillaise. They look down a little on us Italians, since there aren't very many of us who have been in prison or had entanglements with the police, although Tranquillo Agottani was supposedly with the Carbonari. They call a meeting whenever someone has an argument, almost every day. They call their meetings "assemblies" and invite all the other settlers on the ship, except for the Germans, who don't understand French, not many people go. Of us Italians the ones who go most often are Decio, Umberto, Giacomo, and Zeffirino. Decio got in an argument with one of the Frenchmen there whose name is Gorand, but they call him African, because he was in Africa and got a Legion of Honour there. Supposedly Gorand said that the nonexistence of marriage and the sharing of women in our settlement was not intended to gratify our desires, but to cultivate a new generation of children who would combine all their parents' optimal qualities in themselves. Supposedly Umberto said in reply that his optimal quality was that he loves women, and that that was the most important thing for men, otherwise there was no point in establishing a settlement. Gorand said that that was a typical Italian anarchist attitude, at which point Decio inserted himself into the conversation, saying that anarchy was not quite what Gorand imagined it, and that communism was always trying to tell people what to do. Gorand said he had been a communist for eight years and no anarchist was going to tell him what communism was. And he said communism meant love, but not the way Italians and anarchists imagine it. And the first communist was actually Jesus Christ, who was a virgin. Decio said he didn't know Jesus Christ personally, he had only heard about him in church, but from everything he'd heard, Jesus was a downright fool. Wasn't he the one who turned the other cheek when somebody hit him? Gorand said that wasn't the point, they were talking here about love. Then another Frenchman, named Haymard, stepped in, and said Friends, friends, why don't we leave this for another time?

February 16th

The Madeira mountains appeared on the starboard side today. All day long there were birds flying around us. The weather is calm and getting warmer all the time.

February 17th

We crossed paths with a ship. Everyone was shouting and waving their hats and scarves.

Even among us Italians there are disputes over how things should look in the settlement, and gradually three groups have emerged. One led by Zeffirino, one by Decio, and one by no one really—maybe Giacomo. Zeffirino is the richest one of us, or was, anyway, since soon everything will be shared. He pals around with Gorand a lot, since he was in Africa also, and when he returned home after six years, he enrolled in the school of agronomics and worked at the economic commune in Lazio for three years. He was the one who first spread Older Brother's ideas in our country and began talking people into moving away to Brazil. But he doesn't agree with all of Older Brother's ideas. He says it's a mistake for the settlement to be open to anyone, since there are hangers-on and ne'er-do-wells in every group of people, and if our settlement is to be the forerunner of a new world, it should only admit truly capable and motivated individuals. Decio says people aren't born as hangers-on and ne'er-do-wells but become that way through the utter debasement of human labor, and that's the fault of religion and the capitalist system. Giacomo says religion isn't in and of itself counter to freedom, it's possible to believe in a Higher Being and at the same time be a free and full-fledged member of human society. Domenico said a new religion had sprung up in America called the Church of Latter-Day Saints, and that they were establishing settlements and the women were shared, or almost. And that in America they'd found a holy book even older than the Gospels were. Decio replied that everything in America's always the oldest or the newest or the biggest or the greenest, which is typical for fanatics who think they've swallowed Solomon's dung. And as long as people believe in religious claptrap, they'll never be free.

February 19th

We entered the Canary Islands. Most of the ships heading for America stop here to replenish their supplies. The captain said that that would needlessly detain us and it was better to wait for the islands of Cape Verde, and besides, the prices were cheaper there. We crossed paths with two ships.

Mrs. Crisson, who is often ill, was given an unoccupied cabin in first class. Giacomo and most of the Italians and the French say that it's normal and correct. But others say it's a manifestation of individualism and it isn't normal and correct for these sorts of matters to be decided by the husband alone (Mr. Crisson asked the captain about it). Umberto said it was a typical aristocratic move. Elisabetta said that if Mrs. Crisson was sick all the time, she shouldn't have come on the trip in the first place.

We decided with a majority of 30 votes that participation in meetings would be mandatory for everyone, since matters were discussed there that affected all of us. Zeffirino said it wasn't good to let the French discuss everything on their own. We sent a delegation to the Germans and the Austrians, who agreed with our decision, even though almost none of them understand French. Tranquillo Agottani said he would translate into German whatever Decio or Zeffirino or Paolo interpreted into Italian for him. Elisabetta said: Why couldn't Bruno interpret into Italian? Everyone looked at me. We also decided, with a majority of twenty-eight votes, to hold meetings regularly every other evening with the agenda available for participants to look at by 4:00 P.M. at the latest. If there's nothing important to discuss, the agenda will consist of "Singing and Improvised Entertainment." Meetings will be held on deck. Zeffirino asked the captain for a waxed sail for meeting-goers to hide under in case of rain.

February 23rd

Today we had our first meeting. Most of the discussion was about food supplies. The oranges, which are beginning to rot, will be distributed to all the settlers equally, even the Germans, who haven't paid their fees. The sugar will be weighed out and distributed to each as he is owed, but only to those who have turned in their fees. This applies to us Italians, the French, the Austrians, and about a third of the Germans. The motion was submitted by Manfredi, who had noticed some settlers taking advantage of the shared sugar to pour themselves three times more than anyone else.

February 25th

The drinking water is also beginning to spoil. It was agreed to raise the ration of wine per person from 2 dcl to 2.5 dcl. Zeffirino moved that the increase apply only to persons over the age of thirteen, but a group of about twenty Frenchmen, who call themselves Egalitarians, opposed it, so that children will receive the same share as everyone else. Mr. Mangin then moved that volunteers from the ranks of the French hold classes in French for the others, with classes to be held every day before noon on the rear deck. Eight Frenchmen and one Frenchwoman raised their hands to volunteer. We crossed paths with another ship.

February 27th

This morning the mountainous cliffs of the first island of Cape Verde rose up before us. There are ten of them altogether. The captain is heading for the southernmost one, São Tiago. Giacomo read us the encyclopedia entry: a Genoan discovered the island in the fifteenth century. The port we're heading for is called Tarrafal. We should arrive tomorrow afternoon or evening. Cape Verde belongs to Portugal and trades mainly in salt, sand, and slaves. The shipmaster said we might see some whales. There were no meetings or classes held, as people were eager and agitated.

February 28th

We spent the whole day sailing through the islands. We proposed to the captain that we dump the old drinking water and replace it with a fresh supply, but the captain said that water was very expensive in Cape Verde and if we wanted to replace it, it would cost us more than a week's worth of food. Vito Ferroni declared that he didn't see why we hadn't filled up on fresh water when we were in the Canary Islands, where it was free.

Toward evening we dropped anchor at the mouth of a large gulf. People were looking forward to spending a few hours on dry land tomorrow, but the first officer said we'd paid for passage to Brazil, not a tourist excursion to Cape Verde. Decio, Giacomo, and Haymard went to the captain, but he confirmed the officer's words, saying these waters were Portuguese territory and we didn't have permission to leave the ship. But tomorrow morning, he said, local traders would come aboard and we could buy fresh fruit, meat, and bread from them.

March 1st

This morning everyone rushed on deck to wait for the arrival of the Portuguese traders' boats. There was a village at the south end of the gulf with Negro women and children standing in the surf collecting sand from the water and making it into large piles, which the men then carried away on carts drawn by donkeys and animals that looked like buffalo. Other women stood on shore breaking rocks with hammers. I took out my telescope and inspected the inhabitants. The women were stout, almost naked, tattooed, and not very pretty. Thanks to my telescope, I was the first to see the boats rowing toward us from the harbor.

Cape Verdeans don't look Portuguese, they have different traits than Europeans do, and most of them are mestizo. They were selling practically everything, fruit, meat, pigs and fowl, all sorts of tools, even wooden dolls and rattles. I bought six coconuts, two dozen oranges, and a big conch shell for Elisabetta.

Nothing much was discussed at the meeting. We agreed that instead of singing and improvised entertainment, which there was plenty of time for during the day when we had nothing to do, the more educated settlers would hold lectures for the others, and when there was no lecture in store, the older and more experienced settlers would talk about their experiences and how they had come to their worldview. The day after tomorrow, as long as there's nothing more important to deal with, Louis Gabat is going to tell us about the February revolution.

The meeting broke up early and Elisabetta and I went for a stroll on deck. I gave her the conch shell, but nothing came of it.

March 3rd

Louis Gabat comes from the southern Alps, where news of the revolution in Paris had arrived with a two-day delay. The people were happy, he said, and the newspapers wrote that the February revolution was the first step toward the renewal of humanity and the present belonged to the future now. In Digne, where Louis Gabat lived, they held a great celebration for five hundred people. There were two rows of tables with musicians in between and pyramids of rifles and revolutionary banners on either side. The citizens ate and drank and made toasts to the liberation of the world, to the triumph of the people's rights, to putting an end to the past, to equality, to the freedom of all nations. The local priest toasted to fraternity, saying that Christ had raised up the old age into the new age as a token of love and happiness for the whole world. Both of the local newspapers changed their names, the *Alpine Daily* to the *Socialist Daily* and the *Alpine Gleaner* to the *Alpine Republican*. But a few months later, the revolutionary élan had faded away and the citizens' trust was betrayed. The newspapers changed their names back again, the *Alpine Daily* even going so far as to add the subtitle *Fervent friend of the nation and public order*. Louis Gabat made up his mind to join the underground movement that was preparing a new revolution to protect what had been won. In June, he and his friends took over the subprefecture in Forcalquier and were making ready to move on Digne when Marseille sent out the National Guard against them. More than fifty of his companions and his best friend perished in the fratricidal battle. Gabat fled to Paris, where he hid for a while, pondering the question of why his countrymen were killing each other and arriving at the conviction that a fraternal bond was not a bond of blood but a moral one. During that same time he also made up his mind to leave Europe and go work and begin a family in some settlement overseas, where politics and tyranny had not yet come of age.

March 4th

At ten-thirty this morning there was a tragic accident. One of the Negroes, while impregnating the stay lines, tumbled into the sea. The captain had a cutter put in, but it leaked from every side and he declared that to send his sailors out in it would mean their certain death. So the sailors pulled the cutter up and watched the Negro struggle in the waves until he drowned. A sadness reigned on board. The only one who showed no sign of mourning for the Negro was the first officer, who was in fact responsible for his death, since he had sent him to work even though he knew that during the night he had had a high fever. Haymard moved that at tomorrow's meeting we speak about equality among races and the moral unacceptability of slavery and that we extend a special invitation to the two Negro sailors and the cook. The motion was accepted unanimously by those who heard it. Decio moved that we all pitch in for equipment for three people and invite the Negroes to come to the settlement with us and found a new world where it wouldn't be important what race a person was. Zeffirino said that it was a generous motion, but one on which only the assembly could decide (Zeffirino likes to call the meetings assemblies). And that in his opinion inviting the Negroes to join the settlement was at the very least premature and could threaten the outcome of our moral and ideological investment. He said by no means did he intend to excuse the first officer, but on the other hand it was plain that the Negroes didn't exactly break their backs at work. Decio declared that he refused to speak to such an idiot and that he firmly hoped the admission of the Negroes into the settlement would be approved tomorrow.

Samba the cook was the only one of the Negroes who turned up for the meeting that evening, despite that both of the Negro sailors had the night off. He smiled and clapped the whole time. He knew some of the Germans, so he sat with them, saying *Gut, gut,* when they made room for him. Haymard began talking about the origin and history of slavery, but after a few sentences Decio interrupted him and said we all knew what slavery was, old or new, the important thing was not words but deeds. And that he had come to the meeting to submit an important motion. Lecoq and another Frenchman said that there was no mention of it on the agenda and it would be nice if everyone respected the common bylaws. But we Italians began to whistle and the Germans joined in with us, though they weren't exactly sure why, since Agottani hadn't had time to interpret. In the end Decio was allowed to submit his motion. He said we all had plenty of money (some of the Germans cried *Nein, nein!*), and even if some had less than others, it wasn't important, because in a few weeks all of it would be shared anyway, and everyone was welcome to give as much as they saw fit. And he said it would be a great symbol and a triumph of our ideals if we were to admit the scorned and downtrodden Negroes and allow them to become full-fledged members of universal human society. And he sat down. Most people clapped for him, but not everyone. After him Zeffirino got up and said the same thing as yesterday, that it was generous but premature, but he didn't add anything else. Most people clapped for him too. After him a Frenchman got up and said he had nothing at all against Negroes but if we began to make exceptions before we even reached the settlement, it would end up in anarchy. Decio, Paolo, Amilcare, Lorenzo, Alessandro Mansueto, and a few other Italians began clapping and shouting: Long live anarchy! and others whistled and stomped their feet and for several minutes you couldn't understand a thing. Until finally Haymard shouted everyone down and said we weren't here to give everyone a chance to voice their political views, since soon we would all be living as a family. He said personally Decio's motion appealed to him, and suggested we move to a vote, but first we had to be sure everyone knew what we were voting on. He said the question was: Who is in favor of admitting the three Negroes into our settlement and pitching in for their equipment, and he asked me to interpret it clearly and understandably into Italian and Agottani to interpret it clearly and understandably into German. Decio said he also wanted the part about the ideals to be translated. I said there was no point in translating it into Italian, since we had been discussing it among ourselves since morning, but Haymard declared that it had no validity. When it came time to vote, those in favor raised their hands first, and Haymard announced: 88. Then those opposed raised their hands: 20. And when Haymard counted the raised hands, he said that in view of the presence of a majority of more than half the settlers at the meeting and the outcome of the vote, Deci Boni's motion was accepted. I, Elisabetta, Amilcare, Cursio, Egizio, Lorenzo, Umberto, Paolo, Giacomo, Domenico, Pietro Gavarri, Eugenio Grassi, both Alessandros, and the rest of the Italians voted in favor; Zeffirino, Cattina, and Rina were opposed. Samba raised his hand both times, but it didn't matter, since he wasn't a member of the settlement yet at the time of the vote and didn't have voting rights.

March 6th

Today Zeffirino, Durrieu, and Gorand requested a special meeting with the agenda *The Question of the Validity of Yesterday's Voting and Some Questions of Democracy*. But Lecoq and Desmarie, who record the votes and accept the motions, said that the questions could wait until tomorrow. Zeffirino was testy and dissatisfied, he spent the day writing something and in the evening had a long talk with Gorand and a few of the other Frenchmen.

We entered the equatorial regions. The captain is worried about contagion.

March 8th

Even more people came to yesterday's meeting than the last one, but not one of the Negroes. Gorand took the floor and declared that the day before yesterday's vote was invalid, having proceeded in violation of all the rules of democracy and in particular two. For one, Decio's motion had not been placed on the agenda, which meant people hadn't had time to form a considered mature opinion of it in advance. For another, the vote had been open, which may be allowable in common everyday matters, but on fundamental questions only a secret ballot will do, or at least that was his opinion. And those whose mouths were full of democracy should before all else submit to its rules. And for a third thing, it was questionable whether everyone had understood what they were voting on, as testified to by the fact that Samba, without having even been asked, had raised his hand both for and against. Some of our German friends, said Gorand, had had no idea the vote was about the Negroes, believing it to be about providing equipment to those who for lack of financial means had not been able to purchase it in Europe. He demanded that the vote be declared invalid and a new one be held, by secret ballot, with the question written out clearly and trilingually. At which Decio stood up and declared that he didn't see why we were talking about democracy when the issue was helping people in need and that was called brotherhood. And that he was deeply disappointed by some of the settlers' lack of simple humanity. And for that matter that he didn't know who would translate it into German, seeing as Agottani didn't know how to read or write, and he wasn't the only one. And he didn't see what difference it made whether the subject of the vote was expressed orally or written on a piece of paper, which plenty of people wouldn't understand anyway. And that, as far as a secret ballot was concerned, that was in conflict with the ideals of our settlement, where people wouldn't have to hide anything from each other. And that he for one did not intend to hide the fact that Gorand and those like him should have stayed behind in Europe, squatting atop their sacks of gold until their dying day and holding secret ballots every Friday afternoon on whether they should hide the sacks in the barn or in the well.

Decio's speech caused a great uproar, with everyone clapping and whistling and talking over each other, until Lecoq and Desmarie declared the meeting over and said we would meet again today, by which time the more hotblooded meeting-goers should have cooled off. Lecoq said that he hoped everyone would act like adults and responsible members of the settlement and not resort to invective. This afternoon an announcement was hung on the mainmast that in view of the large number of those who wished to speak this evening, no one would be allowed to speak for longer than five minutes and they would take their turns in alphabetical order. Almost all the settlers came to the meeting, even the children. The first to speak, according to alphabetical order, was Decio. He said that he apologized if he had offended anyone yesterday, but he didn't understand how some people could be so thickheaded. He said he didn't know whether our meetings were any use, since instead of solving matters they just complicated them. He said he still considered his motion to admit the Negro sailors and the cook into the settlement a good one, as humanity demanded it. And he said that anyone who didn't understand could go and hang himself. Most of the Italians and the French began to clap, but the Germans didn't know what was going on, since Agottani wasn't able to translate fast enough and they couldn't have heard him anyway. Lecoq rang the bell he had borrowed from the shipmaster, to restore peace and quiet. Everyone quieted down and Agottani began to translate, but then suddenly stopped short and said he didn't know how to say go and hang himself in German. One Frenchman suggested *Gehen in dee shvameh*, but Agottani said that that meant something else. Several people shouted that it wasn't a question of coming up with the exact expression but capturing the meaning as a whole. Decio said he could formulate his thought differently, and anyone who didn't understand could kiss his ass. Lecoq rang the bell and said that Decio Boni no longer had the floor. Decio said that he wasn't finished and still had at least a good three minutes. And that he'd like to know whose floor it was. Umberto began shouting *Viva l'Italia!* and the Italians began clapping. Some of the French joined in with us, sweeping in the Germans, who began clapping and chanting *Viva l'Italia!* along with Umberto. And the accordionist began to play the Marseillaise and the French began to sing and the Italians were crying *Vive la France!* with the Germans repeating it after them. Decio was shouting *Liberté, égalité, fraternité!* Anyone who doesn't understand, go fuck yourself! Lecoq stopped ringing the bell and Zeffirino, Gorand, and about ten other Frenchmen stood up and walked out. The accordionist began to play another song, about a country where there would be no kings or presidents and everything would be shared, and then it went: *No commerce will be allowed, except for casks of wine of course, for wine is something I adore, the color red gives me my strength.* The chorus went: *Wine? Divine! My strength flows from the blood of wine!* and when the French sang the chorus, they would bend their left arm at the elbow and slap it with their right hand and the ladies would grin and giggle. When they were through, they sang Paolo's song about coffee, and after us the Germans sang some long, sad song. Then the accordionist launched into various tunes and Cursio ran for his violin and people began stomping their feet and dancing in place and some clasped hands and danced together. I squeezed through the crowd to Elisabetta and we danced together for at least a half hour. We were sweating like horses.

March 10th

Today Lecoq and Desmarie submitted their resignations and declared that for the time being public assemblies were cancelled. They proposed the election of a five-member presidium that would work out the rules by which the assembly and the voting would be governed next time. Sébastien Durrieu would accept candidacies for membership of the presidium for a period of three days. Elections would be held March 17th and 18th.

One of the Frenchmen came to ask if I could translate a letter into Italian, which he wanted to give to Adelina, and if I could teach him a few sentences. His name is Jean-Loup. He wanted to know how to say: *Where are you from? I'm from Annecy, which is near Italy. Do you have a boyfriend?* And: *Now we are all, so to speak, in the same boat.* He asked if that also had a figurative meaning in Italian.

We are nearing the equator! The thermometer reads 40°. Flying fish leap from the waves. They fly about 50 meters and then drop back into the water. There are fish three or four meters long swimming behind the ship. Some say they're sharks, but other people disagree and say that they are dolphins.

Mrs. Crisson passed away. Mr. Crisson wept and was inconsolable.

It's strange how people's fates collide. Before we left, the only person I really knew was Amilcare, and Cursio and Egizio remotely. And Zeffirino, who published *French for Everyone* in serial form and wrote articles for *Friend of Humanity*. I used to copy them and give them to Amilcare to read. Where did all these people come from? How could people in Germany have found out about the Older Brother project? I asked Agottani about it, he said he hadn't a clue.

Most of the Italians are from Milan and the vicinity, but not all. Agottani is from Naples, but then lived in the north. Apart from a few exceptions, none of them knew each other.

The most organized are the French. A good half of them hail from Savoy and have known each other for some time. The others are from Paris. They used to organize strikes and marches. Some of them have been in prison.

The French who call themselves Egalitarians use a different calendar. Jean-Loup explained to me that according to this calendar, the new year begins in September and the months have different names: Wine-maker, Fog-maker, Frost-maker, Snow-maker, Rain-maker, Wind-maker, Sprout-maker, Blossom-maker, Meadow-maker, Crop-maker, Heat-maker, and Fruit-maker. Today is the 20th of Wind-maker.

Some of us tried to talk Decio into running for the presidium, but Decio said that he wants nothing to do with communists like Zeffirino and Gorand, that communism yokes man with the burden of all that isn't allowed. He said he had nothing against discipline, but discipline has to be the fruit of freedom. He said he was for anarchy and socialism, because anarchy guarantees freedom and socialism a dignified life, and you can't separate the two. Giacomo said that communism and anarchy aren't always completely at odds, it depends on what you can adapt from communism and what you can't, and that he shouldn't be so strict. And that the most important thing is unity, without that we can achieve nothing.

We sailed across the equator and entered the South Seas. The captain had a pig slaughtered, and anyone who has money can buy a piece. The Germans sent a delegation to the Italians and the French, because some of them are completely out of supplies. They're asking us to show solidarity and give them some of our food. The voyage should last another two or three weeks.

March 12th

I wrote a letter to my mother, actually to Padre Francisco in Brescia, who will deliver it and read it to her. In it I wrote about Decio, Elisabetta, the nations of Europe, human races, and flying fish. It's my third letter since the day I left Brescia. I'll send it as soon as we land in Rio de Janeiro.

In the end, Zeffirino was the only one to submit his name for the presidium. He tried to persuade Gorand to do it, but Gorand refused.

Lecoq, Desmarie, and Durrieu issued a joint proclamation saying that due to a lack of candidates, elections to the presidium would be postponed and anyone interested could still sign up today or tomorrow. If no one signs up, the five oldest settlers will be appointed to the presidium.

This afternoon we spotted a raft in the waves. It was built out of two ten- or twelve-meter-long beams and some transom beams. The captain thinks the raft came from a ship that caught fire. The castaways were probably washed away by the waves. This evening the captain called the crew and passengers together to read us the list of anti-fire measures and warned us to pay more attention to them. He also asked the passengers to fill the empty casks of drinking water with seawater. The crew isn't large enough to be able to do the job, two more sailors are sick.

The Germans had a child, a baby girl. Her name is Hoffnung.

This morning we filled the casks, Italians, French, Germans, both Americans, and the five Slavs, who aren't Serbs, as Decio thought, but Hungarians. We made a chain and handed pails down the line. Some of the Germans are so lazy that after a few pails they walk away to rest and smoke a pipe and send their wives and daughters to take their place.

Lecoq, Desmarie, and Durrieu made an announcement that candidates could still sign up tomorrow.

Samba scalded his hand.

This afternoon an argument broke out between the shipmaster and a group of Germans who wanted to build a fire in the hold so they could heat their food. Finally the shipmaster called in the captain, and he threatened to tie up the Germans.

Lecoq, Desmarie, and Durrieu issued a proclamation saying that if no one had signed up by noontime tomorrow, they would ask every settler over the age of forty to come and tell them their date of birth.

About a half hour before noon, all the Egalitarians came to Durrieu and announced their candidacy for the presidium. There are twenty-two of them, with Zeffirino that makes twenty-three candidates. Zeffirino spent all afternoon circulating among the Italians, trying to persuade us to vote for him, since otherwise the whole presidium will be French. He even went to Decio, but Decio said that for him the deciding factor wasn't whether the person was Italian or French, but whether he had brains in his head or mush. Elisabetta said she was going to vote for

Zeffirino. Gorand and the other Frenchmen said they weren't going to vote at all.

Hoffnung has nothing to drink, her mother Katharina has no milk, she's weak and thin. From our shared supplies we set aside the last dates, potatoes, and smoked meat, but she throws everything up right away. Finally, the first officer, who also serves as ship doctor, went below decks to see her, but he barely looked at her, he didn't even raise her eyelids. He just shrugged his shoulders and said there was no remedy for undernourishment, and recommended that she spend as much time as possible on deck in the fresh air. Luigi and Amilcare, along with two of the Germans, took apart one of the bulkheads, asked for a piece of canvas from the shipmaster and made a stretcher out of it. Katharina has two other children as well, both little girls, one three, the other five. Her husband, Helmuth, is a tanner by trade.

March 17th

Zeffirino called off his candidacy in the end. Only thirty-five people turned out for the elections. The Egalitarians called a meeting for tomorrow. During the night a storm broke out, the masts creaked and the lights at the top of the masts went out. In the morning there were dead birds floating in the waves. The Germans tried to scoop them up, but didn't have much luck.

Elisabetta goes to French class every day and knows several sentences now: *My name is Elisabetta, I speak a little French, French is the most beautiful language in the world*, and *Men are born and remain free and have equal rights*. In the evening we go over the sentences together and I correct her and teach her new ones. She mixes up the genders, and so far she speaks only in the present tense: *Yesterday I eat potatoes, When I'm little, I have more long hair*, and so on.

March 19th

Fewer people came to the meeting than usual. Zeffirino and Gorand didn't come. Fifteen or twenty of the French were missing, and even more of the Germans. There were more Italians than anyone else. The Slavs came for the first time, after beginning to speak German all of a sudden out of nowhere when they were helping us fill the casks. The names of the Egalitarians elected were Allegret (Jean and Roland), Penot, Roche, and Dumas. They're all young and wear their hair long, a little like aristocrats and some of the anarchists. Jean and Roland are twins.

Dumas took the floor and declared that the reason he and his friends had stood for the presidium was to salvage what could still be salvaged. He said that the journey was nearing its end and that it would be a good idea to clarify some matters before we embarked on the second leg of the voyage. That some of the settlers, as had come to light in recent days, didn't wish to continue in the journey to Fraternitas and intended to settle in Rio de Janeiro or to depart for Argentina or the United States. And that it would be a good idea to question each of the settlers individually and clarify who stood where. Once we knew who didn't wish to continue on the journey, we would set aside their supplies and the sum to which they were entitled from the shared treasury. The rest of us, on the other hand, would surrender our private funds and belongings to joint administration before we landed, so that it would be clear whom we could actually count on. He and his friends had drawn up a pledge of honor, which each of us had to sign before setting out on the overland journey. Those who didn't know how to write could authorize someone else to sign on their behalf. All matters would be decided by public vote without regard to whether or not the question had been placed on the agenda in advance. In the case of a tie, the vote would be decided by lots. All settlers aged thirteen years and above were allowed to vote, the votes of those under thirteen would be cast by their parents or, assuming they could speak, an individual chosen by the young settlers. Further they proposed that participation in meetings from now on be truly obligatory, so that no one could say they didn't know what we had agreed on. If someone missed a meeting and didn't have a serious reason (illness), the next day he would get nothing to eat. The second time he would be put in isolation from the collective for twenty-four hours, the third time he would be expelled from the settlement.

Dumas said that assuming we agreed to the proposals, tomorrow he and his friends would put together a new list of settlers and then in the evening they would read the pledge of honor. Anyone not present or not wishing to sign would be crossed off the list. At which point we would proceed to the apportioning of shared property. The following day, meaning the day after tomorrow, we would know finally who was in and who was out and could move ahead with settling more important matters.

He said that if this proposal failed to meet with the agreement of those present, he didn't know what else he could offer our collective, and this evening he would hand in a resignation on behalf of himself and his friends. And he concluded: Long live the free settlement Fraternitas, long live brotherhood among nations, I thank you all.

Dumas's speech lasted a long time, since I had to translate everything into Italian, followed by Agottani translating into German. When we were finished, there was a moment of silence and no one said a word. Finally Desmarie spoke up to say that he personally found the Egalitarians' proposals inspiring, albeit with the proviso that they be valid only until such time as we had reached the settlement, at which point the Regulations proposed by Older Brother would take full effect and any eventual alterations or modifications would have to be consulted with him in advance. With that Decio said that he didn't wish to get ahead of events, but to consult everything with Older Brother was unrealistic, seeing as he had visited the settlement only once so far, and to write him in Europe and wait for an answer about everything was not really possible. We were the ones who were going to live in the settlement, after all, and we needed to be able to agree among ourselves. To which Dumas said that this discussion was truly premature, the point was to impose some sort of order on the collective now, not in a month from now. Decio declared that he didn't like the way the food had been handled, that denying people food was undignified. Dumas said that of course it could be discussed, but not for too long, since otherwise, as usual, they wouldn't get anywhere. Domenico suggested that in that case they be expelled straightaway but first they get something to eat. Argia asked whether a woman having her period would be considered an illness. Dumas said they hadn't considered it in such detail, but it could be addressed on a case-by-case basis. One of the Germans spoke up to say that his wife suffered periods of madness. Dumas said that he didn't see what that had to do with it. The German replied he thought that's what the Italian lady had said. Argia said that she was no lady. Agottani said that the German hadn't said any such thing, he didn't say *dame*, but *frau*, which just meant any woman in general, but he, Agottani, had translated it as *signora*. Argia said that just because she was no lady didn't mean she was just any woman in general. And that she had asked her question on behalf of all the women, including the Germans. Dumas said that he had already answered Argia, and Umberto said that women should stay at home when they had their period, everyone was better off that way, not only them. The German said he hadn't meant to offend the Italian frau, and Cattina said that was a typical male remark. The German said he didn't see what was so typically male about it, and Umberto told him not to worry. Cattina said she didn't mean him, she meant Umberto, and Umberto said, What did I tell you, and laughed out loud. By that time I had stopped translating, so Dumas asked what they were talking about and what was so funny, he could use a laugh himself. I said there had been a misunderstanding which led to a comical outcome. Dumas said, Oh I see, but he looked disgruntled, and Roland Allegret said that once everyone had had their fill of laughing, maybe we could get back to more important matters.

Decio declared that the idea of going around to everyone, refunding money to those who had changed their minds and creating a joint treasury for the rest seemed fine to him, but he was opposed to signing a pledge of honor and especially to sanctions for those who missed a meeting. If someone missed a meeting they lost their vote and that was it. Dumas replied that, unfortunately, experience had shown that when someone missed a meeting it didn't mean they didn't still want a say in everything come the next day. And how was Decio supposed to tell the difference between people who had a serious reason for missing a meeting and people who just didn't feel like it? Giacomo suggested that anyone who missed a meeting, whatever the reason might be, could delegate their vote to someone else. Dumas said in theory that seemed reasonable, but it would cause all sorts of confusion and the question was whether there hadn't been enough confusion already. He said he thought a little discipline wouldn't hurt, but on the other hand of course he didn't want to force anything through without the consent of the majority, and we should move to a vote. Everyone looked around, but it seemed no one much cared to vote. Roland Allegret said that maybe it would be better if we took the Egalitarians' motions one at a time instead of all at once, and who was in favor of that. Most people raised their hands. With that one of the Slavs stood up and said that he and his companions did not wish to shirk their obligation to vote but they did not understand what was this settlement we were talking about, and could we explain to them what Fraternitas is. He and his companions had suffered the chains of Austria and Hungary and had decided to go to Brazil in search of gold, which they would then send back to their friends who remained, so they could break their chains, and they needed money for revolvers and a free press. He and his companions were in favor of freedom for all nations and opposed to tyranny. People were clapping and shouting Bravo! Bravo! but Dumas looked even more disgruntled than before. One of the Austrians said that he was ashamed to be an Austrian, for his country had brought whole nations under its yoke, including Hungary, but it wouldn't be long before all people would be free. Umberto said that no one could be blamed for where they were born, and Vito Ferroni said that borders were an invention of capital and the bourgeoisie. Roland Allegret said that he welcomed our Slavic guests, but unfortunately they could not take part in the vote, since that was a right reserved for settlers. But after the meeting he would be glad to explain everything to them, and if they wanted to become settlers, surely no one would have any objection to that. To which Decio said, What ever happened to admitting the Negroes? Roland Allegret said we would deal with that the day after tomorrow, once we clarified the issues that had been raised by his friend Dumas, and the Slavic fellow asked whether there were Negroes in our settlement and why. Decio declared that he had nothing against admitting the Slavs, but the Negroes were here first. Jean Allegret asked whether Decio was sure that the Negroes even wanted to be admitted to the settlement. Haymard said that he had tried to talk with them about it, but the Negroes spoke only English. He asked whether anyone knew English, but no one volunteered. Decio said we could ask the captain to convey our invitation to the Negroes, but Haymard declared that that would be against the captain's interests, since if nothing else he was still going to need the Negroes to load the ship for the passage back to Europe. Decio said that in that case we should turn to our two American passengers for help, but Haymard said he had tried that, but the Americans only spoke English, just like the Negroes.

March 20th

The meeting dragged on into the night, but in the end we managed to pass most of the items. Penot, one of the Egalitarians, who supposedly used to be a clerk in a law office, kept a record of the voting:

Present: about 130 (children included).
Drawing up of new list of settlers:
For: 87, against: 8, abstained: about 40.
Passed.
Surrender of private funds to shared treasury:
For: 55, against: 42, abstained: 30 to 40.
Passed.
Drafting of pledge of honor and signing of same:
For: 65, against: 32, abstained: about 40.
Passed.
Voting age 13 and over:

For: 54, against: 31, abstained: about 50.

Passed.

Vote by chosen delegates for those under 13:

For: 41, against: 54, abstained: 30 to 40.

Drawing of lots in case of tie:

For: 91, against: 2, abstained: less than 40.

Passed.

Option to vote on questions not stated on agenda:

For: 64, against: 14, abstained: 50 to 60.

Passed.

Sanction for unexcused absence from assembly:

For: 86, against: 30, abstained: 10 to 20.

Passed.

Sanction for first absence—denial of food for 24 hours:

For: 45, against: 78, abstained: about 10.

Expulsion from collective for 24 hours:

For: 60, against: 68, abstained: 5 to 7.

Reprimand:

For: 96, against: 7, abstained: about 30.

Passed.

Sanction for second absence—expulsion from collective for 24 hours:

For: 62, against: 66, abstained: 5 to 7.

Second reprimand:

For: 83, against: 18, abstained: 30 to 40.

Passed.

Sanction for third absence—expulsion from collective for 24 hours:

For: 55, against: 66, abstained: about 10.

Third reprimand:

For: 52, against: 66, abstained: 15 to 20.
Expulsion from settlement:
For: 81, against: 22, abstained: about 30.
Passed.
Considered as sound reason for absence—illness or serious injury:
For: 88, against: 2, abstained: 30 to 40.
Passed.
Minor injury or sudden fatigue:
For: 65, against: 35, abstained: 30 to 40.
Passed.
Menstruation:
For: 62, against: 3, abstained: about 70.
Passed.

I spent all day polling the settlers with Dumas, the Allegret brothers, and Agottani. The meeting was postponed. Mr. Crisson loaned me a book his wife wrote. It was published in Paris, but had been banned and wasn't allowed to be sold.

March 21st

Twenty Frenchmen and thirteen Germans intend to settle elsewhere. On the other hand, all the Italians with the exception of Domenico Parodi want to continue the journey to Fraternitas. Domenico has become close with one of the German families and wants to go to the United States with them. There are now 141 settlers altogether. The Slavs have asked for a day to think it over. They explained to us that they aren't Hungarians but Slovaks; Hungarians aren't Slavs, they said, but occupiers. According to them, the Slovaks settled the territory first, along with the other Slavs, who have the oldest language in the world, apart from perhaps the Jewish one, which is why they are called Slavs, from the word *slovo*, meaning "word." And it won't be long before the Slavs break the chains of Austria and Hungary, and the Slavic tongue will sound throughout Europe, in Paris and Berlin, under palace ceilings and in destitute garret flats.

We're nearing Brazil! According to the captain we should be coming within view of it tomorrow or maybe even today. Then less than a week of sailing along the coast awaits us until we reach Rio de Janeiro.

March 22nd

The Brazilian coast lies off our starboard bow, the cape of São Roque. We're heading south. The captain had a pig slaughtered. But he doesn't want to drop anchor, even though the water's almost impossible to swallow, you have to hold your nose and drink it down as quickly as possible.

I told Decio what the Slavs said, it made him angry. He said that, next to religion, patriotism is the greatest pack of nonsense there is. Both lead to the manipulation of human emotions, he said, to unfreedom and intolerance.

Katharina is still throwing up most of her food.

The pledge of honor is still not done. The Egalitarians are try-ing to revise it so that as many people as possible will sign it. Decio announced right from the outset that he wouldn't sign, because all pledges of honor are the first step toward the loss of personal freedom and the exercise of personal discretion. And he appealed to every true anarchist not to sign either. A lot of Italians agree with him, including some who originally voted in favor of it.

I think it will be signed all the same. People are tired of meet-ings and debating regulations, they're both impatient and glad that the voyage is coming to an end. Everyone walks the deck all day, squirting water at one another, singing and joking.

We the people without a name, free of the hatred and malice due to which others acquire a name, we the people without ill will... In times of suffering we have suffered, in times of worry we have worried, in times of torment we have been tormented with humiliation, fear, and uncertainty. We have seen many wicked things around us and we

are exhausted, drained; we have become innumerable. Those who
scorn us have acquired dominion over us; we have bowed down
before them, hoping for compassion; but those who scorn us have
shown no compassion. We turned to our rulers, asking them to put
an end to our suffering and torment, but our rulers did not want
to listen, instead helping those who robbed and devoured us, and
caused us to be diminished. We had but two choices left: to kill the
rulers and become rulers, to acquire a name and torment others,
or to flee and take shelter among the nameless. Here we are among
our own.

March 26th

Giacomo said that *Slav* is not from the word *slovo*, meaning
"word," but from the old Italian word *sclavo*, meaning "slave."

March 27th

I actually know very little about anarchy: that a man must remain free at all costs, that he should refuse to be conscripted
into the army, and that marriage is neither necessary nor needed
and free love is more dignified for man and woman alike. And
that there is actually no such thing as authority, it's only a con-
vention. But I still don't quite understand what freedom of man
is. Or how to achieve that freedom. Decio said even the anarchists aren't of one mind about it. Some say that anarchy is an

intellectual movement while others say that it's mainly a movement of action. And still others say that it isn't a movement at all, but an individual stance. Some think that it's possible to change society in such a way that more and more people adopt an anarchist stance and achieve freedom of thought and thereby form their own opinions of society, politics, religion, and so forth, and that that will lead to the breakdown of traditional society and the creation of a new one in which free people respect other free people. But others believe that that won't happen by itself, that one has to incite chaos and anarchy and the breakdown of institutions, and only then will those who aren't anarchists recognize that another world is possible and see that the government serves only to satiate the pathological ambition of fools who compensate for their own lack of individual freedom by depriving others of it, because those who out of cowardice or timidity have no authority over themselves seek to have it over their fellow citizens. He (Decio) said he didn't believe that one had to commit assassinations and provoke chaos, that it was enough for people to cease to be afraid and they would insist on their rights. And that really the best thing would be if all the anarchists and those who sympathized with them would establish settlements all over the world where there was no authority and people could develop in harmony and freedom, because everyone's opinion would be respected, and people who lived in countries where there *are* governments would simply cease obeying them.

But if every opinion is equally valid, how do you decide? Even for the idea that it's the majority who decides, there had to be someone, some scholar or philosopher, who came to that conclusion, and whoever came to that conclusion first was at that moment the only one who thought so. And I've noticed another thing, too: people who think they're free never agree on anything, while people who don't, almost always agree on everything.

And how can I tell whether I'm free? If I refuse to be conscripted into the army and kill people who've done nothing to me, that still doesn't mean I'm free. Poor people have no reason to kill other poor people, that stands to reason, it even says so in the Bible. But Decio says that religion is the very thing that laid the foundations of the unfreedom which people live in today. He also says that it will be a long time before people cease to believe in religion, and that there are only a handful of people today who don't believe in God. But that would mean most people, or at least most unfree people, are wrong. But how can a person say he's free if he can't persuade somebody else that he could be free as well?

March 28th

Yes, one morning we discovered that people were biting and eating and hating one another, and they had been all along. Let us not be people, we said to ourselves, let us be trees, let us be the shadow of branches, let us be worms. Let us be naked, let us found an empire of the naked, let us be transparent and without fear.

We dropped anchor in view of the port after noon. Tomorrow we set foot on Brazilian soil. Paolo wrote a song called "Brazil." We will never return to Europe again. The sea here is brighter than in Italy.

March 30th

The landing took place amid terrible confusion. To begin with, people wanted the crates of tools they had brought with them out of the storage, but the first officer turned them away, saying that was what the Negroes were for. Then, when we stepped on shore, the Brazilian police stopped us, divided us into two groups, men in one and women and children in the other, confiscated our things, and took us into a plankboard hangar where we all had to strip naked and give them the clothes we had on. We tread in place there naked as worms for three or four hours before they returned them. They stank of disinfectant, and each piece of clothing had a round blue stamp on it saying Controle higiênico, porte Rio de Janeiro. They did the same thing with the clothes we had in our bags. My telescope was stolen. For the next two nights we're going to sleep at the Ilha das Flores inn; the French, the Austrians, and a group of Germans at the Hospedaria dos Imigrantes; and the rest of the Germans in the convent. The coast is thick with peddlers and porters shouting in Portuguese and French: Hotel Imperial! Cleanest sheets in Rio! Pipes! Tobacco! Onions! Castor oil! Brazil has four million citizens and two millon Negro slaves. Nobody knows how many Indians there are. The day after tomorrow we will be transported by boat to Paranaguá, where we will transfer to a train to Curitiba. There we will supposedly get official permission to settle in the district. It's a pity about the telescope, I could have used it to observe the landscape and the animals. The trip from Curitiba is less than a hundred kilometers, which we should be able to cover by stagecoach in three days.

March 31st

Aniceto read us a letter that his cousin sent him for New Year's from the Fraternitas in Rio. It said: "Free settlement Fraternitas January 2nd. Everything is coming along beautifully. The water is outstanding. We haven't come across any wild animals yet, except for a monkey, which a hunter friend of mine shot. To eat we have birds, rice, beans, and polenta. We have to buy bread, but as soon as we have a moment free, we're going to build an oven."

Zeffirino organized a march through the city, with about seventy people in it, men, women, and children, marching in columns of three with tools on their shoulders. They marched down the main street all the way to the emperor's palace, singing songs about labor. In front of the palace Zeffirino delivered an impassioned speech in which he said the settlers were freedom lovers who had escaped the prison of civilization in order to return dignity to human labor and install a government of liberation of man in Brazil. Afterwards, at the inn, he passed around a copy of the speech. Decio made some caustic remarks, asking what a government of liberation of man was and whether Zeffirino intended to install it himself.

I asked Giacomo what he thought about freedom and how soon it could be installed. He said he thought it could be installed once science had revealed the laws of nature. Once we knew the laws of nature, there would be no need for others, which are always in conflict with nature's because they don't derive from the true needs of man. Then, he said, the problem of freedom would be solved. No one could claim any more that hierarchy, political administration, or leadership were necessary for life in society. All those things are despotic, being forced on men by other men and not by nature. Man submits to natural laws and that's all there is to it.

April 1st

Yesterday (evening) in the Hospedaria dos Imigrantes was the last meeting of our settler's group. The Egalitarians submitted a list of those who wish to continue the journey, but some people announced that they had changed their minds and asked for their money back.

OCTOBER 1855

October 15th. I stopped keeping a journal when we arrived in Brazil, even though originally I had planned to continue, but Giacomo Zerla persuaded me to take it up again; he said one day it would be an important testament. This is our sixth month in the settlement now, but the truth is I don't know where to begin. I'm not sure that today is October 15th. October 15th my mother was born. Now that we've reached our destination, people are testy and argue more than they did on the ship. I wrote her a letter, when I get to Guaragi I'll send it. She was born in Casalvieri, not far from Rome. Or I'll tell someone. There is a flagpole in the courtyard flying a red-and-black flag. In the end our departure from Rio was delayed for two days. The evening before that was the last meeting of our group, the Egalitarians submitted a list of those who wished to continue the journey, but some of the settlers announced that they had changed their minds and asked for their money back from the shared treasury. Along the way Decio also managed to get into an argument with Gorand, who said that we would need to elect a provisional leader for the settlement or at least a head manager. The courtyard is what we call the space between the buildings where the road widens out. There are thirty-eight buildings in the settlement, each one with two or three rooms, divided by plankboard walls, but without doors. The buildings are made of logs, with slanted roofs covered with branches. Instead of windows we have sliding shutters that only open halfway, and when it's windy they slam against the wall and make a racket. There's also a Common House, a workshop, a tannery, and a school. Some 170 settlers live here, only fifty-eight from our group came in the end, most stayed in Rio, saying they still needed to give it some thought, some settled in Curitiba or Paranaguá. To which Decio said that he believed in freedom and spontaneous will and that communists didn't know s— about spontaneous will. Gorand said that spontaneous will had to be channeled to result in something rational. And that no revolution could do without rational leadership. To which Decio said that that was the kind of thinking he had fled Europe to escape. Gorand replied that that was his problem, no one was stopping him from going back. And Decio screamed You imbecile! and Gorand screamed You anarchist clod! and Decio screamed Despot! Donkey turd! Cow scrotum! and Gorand screamed Political dwarf! Cripple! Individualist! Originally there was also a plan for a small printing press, to be used to put out a newsletter, but there isn't even money for liquor and tools, never mind a printing press. When we were still in Rio, Zeffirino wrote a long introduction for the first issue, stitched it into a notebook, and circulated it among the settlers for a while, and asked that it be read in school. "At this time of year, when life in the country is bursting with green, when singing and laughter sound from every corner, when the soil is coated with the first pledges of harvest, when the pupa bursts and the butterfly doesn't know where to leap first, here, in mother nature's womb, surrounded by an inhuman world of industry and capital, where people starve and weep, here, in this place and at this instant, begins another world, a world of freedom and prosperity." Then there was something about fish in clear stream waters and how yesterday marked the grand opening of the new printing press, and that this was the first introduction to the first issue, still smelling of printer's ink. When we first arrived, some of the local inhabitants treated us kindly, but some didn't even give us a proper greeting. The ones who gave us the cold shoulder are opposed to any more people coming to the settlement. They say that Older Brother knows about all our problems and still he continues to round up settlers. They say that it's because for every immigrant who comes here, he gets money from the Brazilian government. Some of the older settlers, most of whom come from the vicinity of Parma and used to work in agriculture, claim that our group is too large and not enough of us are familiar with agricultural work, they say what good does a locksmith or bricklayer do us and what use are workers who have never so much as smelled dirt in their lives and the second it begins to rain complain of pain in their joints. Also they say we didn't bring enough tools or women and we interfere in everything and constantly make suggestions. I teach school half the day and in the afternoon work in the workshops.

The school stands off to the side, 300 or 400 meters from the courtyard. There are twenty-five pupils, aged five to twelve. Classes are taught in French even though most of the settlers are Italians. I teach them to read and write and do arithmetic. Germaine Minne teaches geography, her husband died before we arrived, he taught political history. Of the first group of colonists that settled here two and a half years ago, half are left, about fifteen people. They issued new regulations and banned alcohol and tobacco, because alcohol is the scourge of the working man and tobacco a vice that diminishes the work drive and causes fires. Fires have broken out in the settlement twice now, once when lightning hit the granary, and once from someone smoking a pipe. Most of the people who left stayed in America, but two families supposedly returned to Italy. The others, most of them German, left for another free settlement one and a half days' travel from here, called Trautes Heim. To the west lies still another, a more religious one, called Communia. They sent us a delegation to complain that our people were hunting on their land and spreading bad habits. No one observes the smoking ban and there's plenty of tobacco, the Indians bring it in to us in exchange for all sorts of things, buttons, toys, shirts; but with alcohol it's harder, because that has to be bought in the city and the money is shared. The Indians don't smoke or sniff tobacco, they grind it up and put it on their gums and suck the juice. The delegation from Communia was dressed all in black, they had clean clothes and asked to speak to the settlement's board of directors, but Luigi told them we were anarchists and everyone was the board. Also three Brazilian constables came to the settlement. They said that in February the Brazilian police detained a group of former settlers who were ready to confess to theft and robbery in Paranapiacaba district. A search of their homes turned up stolen cotton, furniture, bottles of wine, and so on. The police arrested six men and two women, but the bandits' leader, Arnaldo Socco, managed to escape. The police warned us that if Socco sought refuge in the settlement, it was our responsibility to notify the officials immediately. Otherwise we would all be accomplices. Luigi says that based on the timing of ships from Europe to Rio de Janeiro, we soon should be getting more friends, both male and female. Especially female, he says. The older settlers said there's supposedly another settlement even farther west, founded by vegetarians who came here from Kansas. Vegetarians are people who don't eat meat. Mr. Crisson said that that flew in the face of medical science, which, on the contrary, recommends eating lots of meat. We also have one former lay brother in the settlement, his name is Marco, but for a long time we weren't aware of it, since our settlement is free and against all forms of religion. Most of the Egalitarians left the settlement after five or six weeks, only the Allegret brothers have stayed. Jean is having relations with Elisabetta, but she said she would also sleep with me, but first she had to get used to it. Mr. Crisson also finally left. He intended to settle in California, where supposedly a lot of Frenchmen live. The consumption of meat builds fortitude and strength, and the industriousness of several nations—the Americans, the French, the Dutch, and the English—derives from the frequent eating of meat. October is one of the worst months here, people suffer from fevers. There is also a shelf in the Common House with the word LIBRARY written above it in chalk. The books on the shelf are assorted, most of them are French, *The New Heloise* by Jean-Jacques Rousseau, the *Declaration of the Rights of Man and of the Citizen*, Etienne Cabet's *Voyage to Icaria* in two parts, *The Year 2440* by Sébastien Mercier, a bound volume of the weekly *Under Cover*, a novel called *I Have Loved and Been Loved* (no author), some agricultural guides, and so on. Three or four books are in German, and there is one in Italian, *Anarchists: The Perspective of a Mental Doctor* by Dr. Cesar Lombardi. Originally Giacomo put his three-volume dictionary in the library, but after one of the volumes went missing, he took back the remaining two. The communists hold meetings and bicker about what should be done. Elisabetta and I still talk about a new life, but it's different than it was on the ship. Sometimes she strokes my cheek, but when I try to touch her breasts or in between her legs, she says: No, Bruno, not yet. She doesn't say when, only "not yet." I think that free love is useless unless it's put into practice. Decio sees the main problem in the fact that the settlement has far more men than women and that most of the women suffer from old prejudices and reject polyandry. The married women selfishly stick to their husbands and families and only rarely are they willing to get together with anyone else. On the other hand, those who are single have two or three partners at most, and instead of devoting themselves to them equally, they play the coquette, inciting jealousy. Also the men who have steady partners only reluctantly loan them to others, and despite not having the courage to object to anything publicly, afterwards they snap at them at home. Decio said that he had given the matter some thought and we ought to try inviting some Indian women into the settlement. And we should set up a distillery and produce liquor, not for us, but for the Indian chiefs, who in return would grant their surplus young women to us. Marco said: You mean you want to *buy* them? Decio said: Do you have a better idea? And he said the Indian women would be freer here than they are with their own people and it wouldn't take long for them to become full-fledged settlers, even freer than most of our women, since they don't have any bourgeois prejudices. Marco said: As in the end justifies the means? Marco was originally a sheep shearer and day laborer, but then he had emigrated to France and settled in Lyons, where he took part in an anarchist uprising and fought against martial law, and for that he was condemned to seven years in prison. There was a priest who used to come to the prison. Marco refused to see him at first, but then the other prisoners told him that the priest was smuggling tobacco into the prison and handing it out after confession. So Marco signed up for confession, but the priest told him flat out, Son, I know you only signed up for the tobacco, here's a fistful and you don't have to confess, I seek to persuade by words, not by earthly goods. With that the two of them got to talking and the priest asked where he was born and so on, and speaking of justice and hope, and Marco liked it, so the next Sunday he signed up again, took the tobacco, and had a chat with the priest. As the weeks went by, Marco began to take an interest in faith, and learned to read and write, and eventually he read the Gospel and decided to devote his life to Christ and help the poor and oppressed, he even joined the Franciscans, but after a few months he quit the monastery and joined up with a group of emigrants. And that brought him here. Decio liked to make fun of Marco, asking him what he thought of our Sodom and Gomorrah. And never mind us, what about the Indians who were living out of wedlock and didn't even know it, shouldn't they be evangelized? Marco says that the difference between him and Decio is that he loves all people in their imperfect humanity, while Decio loves what people could be but scorns what they are; whereas Decio says that life is like a big theater, and if he doesn't like what's playing, he has the right to walk out and slam the door, even if it disturbs the others who are happy with the performance. The Negroes didn't join us in the end and instead returned to the ship, even after Decio explained that in the settlement they would be free and said the words *Freedom, freedom.* The Slavs went off in search of gold for their revolt against the Hungarians. When we landed at Rio, it turned out that one of the Slavs was a young woman, the sister of one of the men, she had her hair cut short and didn't speak. Jean Allegret said that women were the future of humanity, because they give life and have a greater sense of unity and harmony and are peace-loving by nature, whereas men seek to disrupt harmony, and that leads to wars and destruction. Umberto tapped his forehead and said that if women were peace-loving, then he was the pope. Mr. Crisson said that a man's brain weighs an average of 1,400 grams, whereas a woman's just 1,300, and Elisabetta said that Umberto's brain weighed ten at most, but Cattina said that Umberto had more sense than all the men put together, including Mr. Crisson. Each settler is entitled to 250 grams of meat a week, children under twelve are entitled to 100. Our money is dwindling and we haven't thought of a way to earn any yet, except for the sale of livestock and hats at the Guaragi market, but there isn't much livestock either. Zeffirino proposed issuing bonds which we could sell in Europe and Rio de Janeiro and which would be guaranteed by our settlement's ten-year economic plan, and drew up a demographic curve showing how many of us there would be in ten years. The school has signs on the walls, or actually slogans: *All men are brothers. Equality in joy, not in misery. Strength in unity. One for all and all for one. God does not exist, but man does.* Marco requested that the slogan with God be removed, since we don't have any idea whether or not God exists. He presented his request at the evening assembly, which aroused a vehement debate during which it came to light that most of the settlers believed that God didn't exist but there was some sort of Higher Being, since otherwise life would have no meaning, or death. On the other hand some said that only nature existed and it was none of any Higher Being's business. Dorgen (who arrived with the last group) stated that the meaning of human life was given by the being called man, and Decio said that man's life is like a notebook on whose pages we write our own story, and a Higher Being is like a big ink blot on the pages of those who haven't learned to think for themselves. To which Marco said: That's not an argument, that's a metaphor, and Decio said: Naturally. What else is life but a metaphor? Mr. Crisson said that one could doubt the existence of God, it was philosophical, and that freedom lies precisely in the ability to doubt, which is also philosophical. Marco said: I believe that God exists, but I admit I cannot know it with certainty. I know only that I know nothing. Decio said: I on the other hand know that if freedom exists, God does not, and vice versa. We may wager on one or on the other, but not on both. At which Argia inserted herself, saying that if nothing existed, you wouldn't know anything, since you wouldn't be here to say what you knew or didn't know, it's only common sense. Decio said that it was always those without any sense who spoke of common sense, and that these fools all consider anyone who bothers to think about things a madman. Argia got angry and said that Decio was the fool, not her, and that she wasn't the only one who thought so, Livia and Francesca thought so too, since in spite of what Decio thought, women could think too. At which point Zeffirino stepped in and said that he was in favor of freedom of belief, that was also a freedom, but some anarchists didn't want to accept that, because they didn't recognize any freedom but their own. Decio said that he had a friend who bought a parrot at the market, and when he brought him home the parrot began to shout Hail Mary!, and asked whether that was also freedom of belief. Zeffirino said that some anarchists had a habit of changing the subject when they ran out of arguments, and it wasn't parrots we were talking about but people, who are gifted with freedom of thought, at which point Mr. Crisson said that according to some naturalists there are also animals gifted with freedom of thought, though he hadn't read anything specifically about parrots. Zeffirino also showed us the plans for the settlement of the Society for New Life from Lyons, according to which they would have a theater, an art gallery, a mill, and a sewage system. Germaine says that we could put on theater and exhibitions in the school or in the open air, but no one feels like it, in spite of the fact that art is useful even in difficult conditions, for it lays bare the passions of man. Last week a fight broke out among the men who work in the field, and one, from the first group of immigrants, pulled a knife and stabbed two of his friends and threatened to kill them. Jean Allegret declared that he had nothing against Elisabetta sleeping with anyone else, providing, of course, she consented. He said he thought the polyandric family was the future of mankind. We owe more than 2,000 réis to suppliers and traders. The oldest pupil in the school is Armanda, who will be twelve soon and is beginning to sprout breasts. I think it might be worth having a talk with her before someone else gets to know her. Before school, the children take care of the livestock, at noontime they have a two-hour break, playing tag or blind man's buff, there are no other games here and at night there's nothing to do. In the afternoon they weave straw hats. Tranquillo Agottani has gotten old, he doesn't want to talk to anyone or do any work, at most he goes to fetch water. When he gets drunk he says, Give me back the sea! Give me back the sea! and swears at everyone. Decio urges complete freedom for everyone, he says no one should be forced to work if they don't want to. The new society has to arise spontaneously. Money is in short supply and some of us are working on the construction of a new road that leads from Caçador to Itararé. It has to be organized from below, by ordinary citizens, whether workers, farmers, or city dwellers, first in groups based on shared interests, then in communities, districts, countries, and eventually in a grand worldwide federation. In this way a free anarchistic order will gradually be achieved in accordance with the interests and the desires of each individual. Mr. Mangin, who is otherwise fairly quiet, said what we had here reminded him of prehistoric times, when people also organized themselves in groups based on shared interests, only the interests were never shared with the shared interests of other groups. And in prehistoric times at least people knew who belonged to which group, whereas in our settlement the groups changed every day, because every time two people began to backbite a third, it ended up in a new group. Mr. Mangin works on the construction of the road and he was the one who found our first casualty, René Collet, who arrived with the last group this summer. We found another two, Gaillac and Torres, in the woods, when after two days they hadn't returned from the hunt, they were lying next to each other with their throats slashed and their arms crossed on their chests. Their muskets were gone. I've never killed anyone. Not even a large animal, like a pig or a goat. Umberto also disappeared out of nowhere one day and couldn't be found, but after five days he came back, bringing two Indian women with him. He took them home and refused to lend them to anyone else. During the day they worked in the tannery, but after two or three weeks they picked up and went back to their people, and when Umberto ran after them, they threw rocks at him. Carlo drowned bringing our two horses to the river. Some say that he was drunk, but others don't believe it and say it was murder too. Various proposals were submitted—call in the constables or hire the Indians, so they could guard our settlement against intruders—but no one knows with certainty who the intruders are and whether there even are any, and turning to the constables would be in conflict with the ideals of our settlement. In the end it was decided to purchase new, more modern muskets. There are also some Germans from Trautes Heim working on the road and Erasmo says that they were the ones who killed his brother, there's no trusting Germans. The Germans from our expedition, who left us, took tools with them which weren't theirs. Three families and twenty more settlers, almost thirty people, are planning to leave. Jean-Loup wants to go to São Paulo and open a shop selling sailor's goods, just as soon as he rounds up the money. Domenico wants to set up a sawmill in Curitiba. Decio says he's going to leave the settlement too, though he doesn't know where to. Puig Mayol walked away from the settlement after cracking open the safe and stealing 500 réis, almost half our money. Gorand proposed establishing a settlement guard, to be governed by a duly and freely elected Council. One of the older settlers, Benito, said in reply that there had already been a Council elected a long time ago, but no one would listen to it. Gorand said, Exactly, if they had a settlement guard, then people would pay more attention to them, because most of the settlers were honest, but not all of them. And honesty isn't an empty word and it alone makes possible firm relationships between people, since then people know what they can expect from others. Desiderio Mezzi, who everyone calls Desimezzi, said that religion had tried something similar, issuing all sorts of precepts and prohibitions, but honest people can do without religion. Marco said nothing to that, but one of the Frenchmen said that honesty was a result of faith in God, not faith in man, and that first there was religion and only after that honesty, because for people to be honest, they have to be afraid. Desimezzi said he didn't agree and it was the other way around, and for that matter people are afraid of all sorts of things. Decio declared that the main thing people should be afraid of is their own stupidity. And Gorand said, Can anyone here be sure that our people weren't killed by the holy rollers from Communia? It wasn't the Indians, they would have run them through with spears or cracked open their heads with a rock, but they wouldn't have cut their throats and crossed their arms on their chests. The crossed arms speak to a certain level of civilization. Benito said that there had been conflicts with Communia from the very beginning, and Cattina said that she, on the other hand, didn't trust vegetarians, because anyone who didn't eat meat must be out of their minds. Just one little piece of freshly grilled meat and it's like your stomach is in heaven.

OCTOBER 1855

October 15th. This is our sixth month here now, but the truth is I don't know where to begin. I'm not sure that today is October 15th. There is a flagpole in the courtyard flying a red-and-black flag. Our departure from Rio was delayed in the end. Now that we've reached our destination, people are testy and argue more than they did on the ship. The courtyard is what we call the space between the buildings where the road widens out. The settlement has thirty-eight log cabins with roofs covered with branches and two or three rooms in each one. We are free, no leaders or political advisers, just as Gorand originally proposed. He stuck around three or four weeks and then one day he left, supposedly he's in another settlement, where they're mostly Germans, called Trautes Heim. But most of our Germans stayed here. The women are shared, even for the Germans and Portuguese, but most of them only want to sleep with one man, seeing as they're equal.

Altogether there are 160 of us, including about 40 children. The children are shared too, and whenever they have a fight with their parents they go and sleep somewhere else. Elisabetta is expecting a child, but we don't know whose it is. Nowadays I live mostly with Germaine Minne, who teaches geography and political history at the school. Besides the school, the settlement also has a Common Home, a well, a distillery, and workshops. The Common Home has a hearth, a table that runs almost all the way across the room, a cabinet with accounting and official documents, dice, cards, chess and checkers, and a shelf of books, most in French. There's only one Italian one, *Anarchists: The Perspective of a Mental Doctor* by Dr. Cesar Lombardi, and several issues of *Atheist*. In the end, only forty-eight people came from our group. There are over a hundred older settlers and eleven Indian women, whom we acquired from the local chiefs in exchange for hard liquor. Zeffirino puts out a settlement newspaper, *The Aware Anarchist*, which he writes up in four copies; one he sends to Europe, one to some newspaper in Rio, one he keeps for himself, and the fourth one circulates among the settlers. Three issues have come out so far. He says it will be an important testament one day. The children go to school fairly irregularly, since they have the same rights as adults and no one can force them to. Zeffirino proposed that school be compulsory for children up to twelve years old, given that education is the pillar of awareness, and that everyone get the same education, given that it solidifies the collective. Decio was opposed, saying that upbringing comes from life, not school, and that having the same education for everyone is an invention of the communists who in reality long only for all people to be the same, and they call that a collective. Zeffirino replied that a collective means an association of people in which people respect one another based on common interests, and for people to have common interests, they have to have a collective upbringing. Zeffirino says that people like Decio aren't true anarchists, they place the individual above society, which is an incorrect interpretation of anarchy, and is actually an expression of aristocratic condescension toward life, and perhaps even decadence. And we have to be circumspect, since anarchy conceived in this way can lead to tyranny and the extinction of civilization. Mr. Crisson said it hadn't been proven that tyranny leads to the extinction of civilization, it may on the contrary contain within itself the germs of a more mature civilization, and in ancient Greece and Rome it was actually in times of tyranny that philosophy bore its most tasteful fruit. The question in fact ought to be posed differently, namely, is civilization necessarily a vehicle for freedom, and one might have doubts about that. The Indian women don't want to alternate partners, they live with only one man, even if sometimes he has two living with him. Zeffirino thinks that care should be taken when having intercourse with the Indians to ensure that the mixing of races remains a marginal phenomenon. He proposed that we also admit some Indian men to the settlement so they could sleep with the women while the white men slept with the white women, but the settlers who lived with Indian women rose up against it. In the end the Negroes declined to join us and insisted on going back to the ship, even though Decio explained that they would be free in the settlement and said the words *Freedom, freedom*. The Slavs went off in search of gold for their revolt against the Hungarians. When we landed at Rio, one of the Slavs turned out to be a young woman, a sister of one of the men, she had her hair cut short and didn't speak. Jean Allegret said that women had a greater sense of harmony and were peace-loving by nature, and that women were the future of humanity, because they give life. Umberto said in reply that he'd like to know how women could give life if not for men, and for that matter men were more important, since in every seed was a viable fruit while not every fruit necessarily had a seed. There are signs up on the walls at school, or actually slogans: *Do what thou wilt, All for all and none for one, Equality in freedom not slavery, Without freedom there is no discipline*, and *Humanity rushes on toward prosperity, peace, women's liberation, anarchy, and harmony*. Two fires have broken out in the settlement, one when lightning struck the granary, the other from someone smoking a pipe. Our living conditions are getting worse, there isn't enough food, and supplies are shrinking daily. Last week we had to slaughter three of our last eleven cows. Jean-Loup and I signed up for a work group which is helping a local firm build a road. Jean-Loup lives with Adelina. We use the money to buy groceries in Palmeira. Ten to fifteen people from our settlement work there every day. There are also people from two other free settlements which also need money. Mr. Mangin also goes with us regularly. He was the one who found our first casualty, René Collet, who arrived with the last group this summer. We buried him in a meadow by the stream, with stones on the grave. Wilhelm also showed interest in Adelina, but Adelina says that she has to get used to it first. Dorgen says that we must overcome this phase, and one can live off ideals and a little bit of polenta. At least temporarily. We receive money from Older Brother in Italy, which he raised through subscriptions in anarchist circles, but it isn't enough. Zeffirino drew up a questionnaire for men and women who have more than one partner. He says that this is a new socialist experiment whose results need to be analyzed and sent to Older Brother in Europe. It has questions such as: *Do you feel abandoned when your partner goes to stay with someone else? Would you prefer two-on-one intercourse (two men, one woman)? Would you be willing to take part in collective intercourse? If your partner has a child, would you be unconcerned with whose it is, or would you try to figure out whether it was yours? Do you think the quality of a child is related to the congenital potential of its parents? Do you think it would be appropriate to assign partners as couples based on their congenital traits?* Respondents may select one of four options: *Yes, No, I don't know, I'd rather not think about it.* Zeffirino also proposed issuing bonds which we could sell in Europe and Rio de Janeiro, guaranteed by our settlement's ten-year economic development plan. Decio declared that Zeffirino was a fool, and Mr. Crisson said that issuing bonds would be capitalistic. Our group is the fifth to have come here from Europe, and one more family arrived after us, a father and mother with five children. Is that all? asked Benito, one of the older settlers, when the family appeared in the courtyard. Well then. Welcome to the Fraternitas free settlement. The four greatest attractions of our settlement are poverty, envy, suspicion, and alcoholism. Welcome, friends, welcome. Their oldest daughter is named Florinda, she's fifteen or sixteen. Luigi said that Benito sees everything too darkly and that he was eroding our pioneering optimism. And that based on the rhythm of ships sailing from Europe and Rio, other friends, both male and female, should be turning up soon. Especially female, Luigi says. It wouldn't take much for the settlers to regain their zest for work, he says, three or four true anarchists would do the trick. He sees the problem as being mainly that there are far more men than women in the settlement and most of them suffer from old prejudices and reject polyandry. Florinda began to flirt with the men right off, but she didn't want to do anything with any of them for a long time. Then all of a sudden she began sleeping with six or seven at once. Some of the men are uneasy about it, and say two or three partners is normal but that seven is too much. Her parents are threatening to leave the settlement. Johann and Kris had a fight over her, Johann accused Kris of knocking the ladder out from under him on purpose while they were building a cabin. Kris said that he didn't even touch the ladder, and that Johann is jealous of him and pulled a knife and stabbed him in the forearm. There isn't any shared entertainment like we used to have on the ship, at best people play cards or checkers, and most of the settlers drink every night, sometimes even during the day. Then come evening they sleep off their hangovers in front of their cabins or by the side of the road and the dogs come and sniff them. Tranquillo Agottani has gotten old, he doesn't want to talk to anyone or do any work, at most he goes to fetch water. When he gets drunk he says, Give me back the sea! Give me back the sea! and swears at everyone. Decio drinks a lot too. One day, drunk, he surprised me and Germaine in bed, and instead of leaving he walked around the room shouting, Just go ahead and screw, screw, screwing is the future of humanity. Carlo drowned bringing the donkeys to the river. Some say that he was drunk too, but others don't believe it and say that it was murder. Then a rumor spread that one of the neighboring settlements was getting ready to attack us and steal our property because something of theirs had gone missing and people there were convinced that the anarchists had done it. Supposedly they call our settlement Sodom. Sodomy is allowed here, but not with animals, since that might unsettle them and the farmers are opposed to it. Mr. Crisson says that when people do it it isn't sodomy but pederasty or sapphism. Most people, though, think that pederasty is against the laws of nature and shouldn't be tolerated in an anarchistic settlement, because anarchy professes to love nature. Mr. Crisson says that it isn't so simple and it hasn't been established whether pederasty exists among animals too or not. And that the presence of pederasty and the degree of tolerance in a society are in fact philosophical problems. Wilhelm disagrees and says the Greek philosophers were opposed to pederasty, and that one of them, Aristotle, described the case of a horse which on seeing pederasts would become so frightened that it rose up on its hind legs and whinnied. Mr. Crisson said he knew that book and it wasn't about pederasty but about parents having intercourse with children, which, unlike pederasty, had been established in nature long ago, Aristotle or no. Umberto said that he would never understand pederasty in his life but he had nothing against sapphism. Nobody knows whether or not the women in the settlement have intercourse together, but Egizio and Primo were supposedly pederasts. Egizio and Primo left the settlement several weeks ago, and most of the Egalitarians are also making ready to leave. Puig Mayol stole 500 réis from the treasury, almost half of our money, and fled. Zeffirino and a group of volunteers gave pursuit, they laid in wait for him outside a pub in Guaragi, tied him up, and dragged him back. I've never killed anyone. Not even a large animal, like a pig or a goat. We bought four new muskets and the Egalitarians submitted a proposal for the sexual reorganization of the settlement. Each man and woman would have only one partner. Couples would be determined by lots, at least until there were enough women in the settlement. Every three months there would be a new lottery. The pederasts could live together in one cabin, but they wouldn't be included in the lottery, as that would be pointless. We were supposed to meet to discuss it the next day, but then the incident with Puig occurred, and we have yet to meet to this day. Each settler is entitled to 120 grams of meat a week, children under twelve are entitled to 50. Our money is dwindling and we haven't thought of a way to earn any yet, except for the occasional sale of handcrafted items at the market in Guaragi and our work on the road. Which has the advantage that we get the money the same day, in the evening after work. Manpower is scarce and it has yet to happen that the foremen have refused anyone, unless they show up late or drunk. We turn our earnings over to Siegfried, who is in charge of the account book, but that often leads to disputes, since some men turn over only part of their money, or go and work for another group on the sly, so that they can keep everything. One day Gian Manni reported that on his way back he had been jumped and had his money stolen, but then it came to light that he had lost it in the casino which the stonecutters from Paranaguá had opened at the construction site. Manni is known as Got-Up-Early-in-the-Evening. A lot of the older settlers are known by nicknames, usually based on some incident. Benito said that it was an Indian custom, and that it had been introduced to the settlement by some German who was known as Scorched Head and who in the end went off to live with the Indians. Some of the settlers I know only by their nicknames, Looked-for-Poppy, Chased Water, Sharp Grass, Can't-Get-It-Up. The other settlers have normal, non-Indian nicknames, Melonhead, Fatso, Jawbone, Gash, She-Dog, and so on. Puig Mayol didn't have any nickname. When they led him through the settlement, a lot of people shook their fists at him and spit on him. The next day there was a trial, which everyone took part in except Decio. Zeffirino proposed the death penalty, since theft may be excusable in the world of capital, where people are exploited, but when a person is free and surrounded by other free citizens, theft is inexcusable, especially given that the settlement needs money for the purchase of tools and seeds, which Puig Mayol knew very well, and in spite of that he committed a crime against our fraternal settlement and thus against all humanity. And he said that he could imagine no greater baseness and that evil must be nipped in the bud, for only in that way was it possible to build a new world. People clapped and shouted, Bravo! Bravo! and it was a long time before they quieted down. Finally Mr. Crisson took the floor and asked that Puig Mayol be granted a counsel for defense, but Zeffirino said there was nothing to defend here, the factual basis of the crime had been proven, and most of the people began to clap all over again. Marco, Luigi, Dorgen, Smala, and a few other settlers tried to shout over them to voice their agreement with Mr. Crisson, but the others whistled and swore at them. Luigi went to fetch Decio, to speak against Zeffirino, but found him completely drunk and unable to utter a sentence. Zeffirino meanwhile proposed that each settler individually state their choice of punishment so that justice would receive its due. A lot of people refused, but others asked to speak and said, Death, I demand death, I vote for death, and Bonifacio said, His sort ought to be crushed like a bedbug, and Cattina said, We aren't going to clasp a viper to our bosom, and Helmuth said, Do we have any choice if we want to go on living in mutual trust? The Egalitarians, who wanted Puig ceremonially expelled from the settlement, were opposed, as were Marco, Luigi, Paolo, Smala, Vito, Mario, Giacomo, Dorgen, Monica Levi, Mr. Crisson and Mr. Mangin, Germaine and I, and another dozen people or so. Peno said, I refuse to share the blame for the death of my brother, and Mr. Mangin said, Let's give him another chance, he's a wretched soul the same as us after all, and Germaine said, If we are free, let us wish freedom unto others, even if they commit an evil deed toward us. A third group of people was undecided and didn't want to vote and Elisabetta said, It's a difficult decision, I really don't know. But the most numerous were those who called for death. Puig Mayol didn't have one true friend in the settlement, he had come by himself and spoke only Portuguese, but he worked with the rest in the workshop and treated people kindly. At one time he had lived with Charlotte, who everyone called Rusty, she had come with her son in the first group, her husband was killed by the national guard, but in the end she left. Zeffirino announced that the result of the voting was clear and that he thanked those who had voted for the strictest sanction and hadn't allowed themselves to be appeased by unconvincing excuses, because humanity is more important than individual human life. Then began a debate about whether the execution should be public and by what means it should be carried out in order to distinguish it from executions in the world of capital. Torres proposed using an Indian method: when an Indian is condemned to death, a council of elders chooses five or six men and they draw lots to see which of them will be the executioner. Then one steps up to the condemned from behind, sticks his fingers in his nostrils, tips his head back, and slits his throat. And someone asked, So who will take this on himself? and everyone was silent. Torres said that we could draw lots like the Indians do, but Aldino said that it was out of the question for him to take part in a lottery and if Torres was so smart, why didn't he slit Mayol's throat himself? Torres said maybe an Indian woman could do it, but one of them said that it was a man's job. Someone objected that women were equal to men in our settlement, and if men washed dishes, then a woman could do a man's work, but the Indian woman got mad and began to scream at him in Indian and the other Indian women joined in and one of them began to sing and one by one all of them broke into song. Zeffirino asked them to stop, but they just sang even louder, and Paolo began to sing a song about brotherhood and we joined in, and when we were done, Penot and Roche began to sing another song, which said that a free man knows no anger, and then some of the Germans began to sing

113

too, and the Indian women clapped along, and then Decio came staggering up and said what were we celebrating and finally there was some fun around here. But while some people sang, others were whistling and shouting, Quiet! and Zeffirino was screaming that it was an attempt at diversion and that such practices were unworthy of democracy.

OCTOBER 1855

October 15th. I stopped keeping a journal when we reached the settlement. This is our sixth month here now, but I don't know where to begin. The vegetable garden has been expanded, a run has been built for the livestock, the agricultural work and manufacture of bricks continues, we're building new homes for the families with children. Some of the settlers complain of the monotonous food and arduous work. People are occasionally testy to one another and there are arguments sometimes. It isn't good for the future of our settlement. Conflicts and disputes are settled in a people's tribunal. The settlers present decide on the sanction. Conflicts, which are called public investigations, take place in the Common House, Carlane from the first group of settlers runs them so everyone doesn't speak at once, supposedly he used to be an adjunct judge. He sits at the head of the room with his back to the window, the parties of the dispute face him and the settlers are on the benches in back. There are red and black flags on the walls. Everything is public, the discussion and the decision as well. It's essential that order reign, since otherwise we wouldn't become the vanguard of a new society. Anarchy is not arbitrariness, and freedom must be answerable to that which makes it possible. But every sanction must be adequately explained, so the guilty party won't persist in his mistake. In the old society people kept things secret, not wanting evil to flow to the surface. But evil suppressed is the source of hatred and individualism. On the contrary it is essential to say everything out loud so that nothing remains hidden. Jean Allegret is entrusted with counting the votes. A hundred settlers live in our settlement, including children. Besides the Common House we have about thirty other buildings, workshops, a granary, a tannery, and a school. In the courtyard in front of the Common House every day at sunset we hold a moment of gathering: the settlers form a circle, clasp each other by the hand, and remain silent until the moment when the sun sets. After that we break up into small groups or pairs and talk about the future. Two fires have broken out in the settlement, one when lightning struck the granary, the other from someone smoking a pipe. Smoking has been forbidden since then, the same as the consumption of alcohol, but some people smoke and drink in secret. The Germans who work on the construction of the road a few kilometers from here sell them tobacco and liquor. They live in a free settlement too, by the name of Trautes Heim, they're allowed to smoke, snort tobacco, and once a week drink alcohol. Zeffirino says that if we want to stop thinking the old way, first we need to change our behavior, rid ourselves of our habits and vices. Individual freedom has been temporarily suspended because it turns out that people aren't ripe for it yet, although it remains our goal in consideration of the fact that it's the first requirement of harmonious development. However, it is important that people first agree on what freedom is, and whether or not the self-will of a few individuals is the expression of true freedom. Anarchy doesn't mean just unthinkingly imitating nature, we must build the foundations of civilization. Shortly before our arrival in the settlement a referendum was held, and a constitution was issued, and a Charter of Obligations. Some settlers objected that anarchy was opposed to all precepts and prohibitions, but the majority decided that it was necessary for people to uphold obligations, because that's the way the groundwork is laid for a new civilization. The draft constitution was approved by a large majority, but Germaine was opposed. Germaine teaches geography and political history in the school and says she would rather leave than have to submit to a dictatorship. Everyone has the right to leave the settlement, but they aren't allowed to take anything with them, since no one is free to cancel their voluntary commitment. To cancel one's voluntary commitment is a crime against us all. I'm not sure whether today is October 15th. Bands of thieves and firebrands roam the area, setting out at dusk and arriving at the gates of the village in the morning, they walk barefoot in single file and tread lightly as cats. Bats as big as mountain eagles live here, they taste like roasted hen. The Indians raise pigs with a dark stripe down their back, dogs, hens, and birds with a big flat beak they use for catching fish. They call them *ayayas*. Their word for knife is *kop* and fishing rod is *poontang*. Elisabetta and I hardly see each other anymore. Last month she lodged a complaint against Umberto, saying that he forced her into unplanned intercourse. Umberto objected that he believed Elisabetta had consented, because when a woman says No, no, she actually means Yes, yes. But Carlane said that maybe that was how it worked in the world of the bourgeoisie, but not in our fraternal society, where everyone, including women, weighs their words and uses them in their original and unambiguous meaning. Umberto declared that he had his doubts, because several women in our fraternal society had originally told him No, no and then were satisfied afterwards. Cattina stood up and said that she could confirm that, and that Elisabetta was a tease who strutted around in front of the men and then acted insulted, and she meant what she said in the original and unambiguous meaning, weighing her words. I felt sorry for Elisabetta, but Germaine agreed with Cattina. But Manfredi, who lives with Cattina now, agreed with Elisabetta and said that maybe Umberto was spreading diseases. Umberto objected that he wasn't spreading diseases and lived a healthy, well-balanced life. Zeffirino wrote a booklet titled *Health for One, Health for All*, which he circulated through the settlement. There is a paragraph in it about venereal diseases and how the settlement can protect against them. There is also a paragraph in it on smoking and alcohol. Under the constitution the women belong to everyone, but in order to avoid problems, an Executive Council decides who they will have intercourse with. But sometimes there are instances of unplanned intercourse. To keep the women from tempting the men, they wear their hair cut short, and as soon the settlement budget will allow it, we're going to purchase cloth to sew the same clothes for all of them. Jealousy will be strictly punished. Jean Allegret said that the measure was directed mainly at men, that women aren't jealous because they have a greater sense of unity and harmony and are peace-loving by nature. Elisabetta broke into tears and Umberto received a second-degree censure. We purchased new muskets and forbade the Indians from wandering around the settlement. When we arrived here, there was a welcoming ceremony during which each of us got a settlement scarf, men black and women red. Some members of the settlement don't wear them. Decio stayed in the settlement five weeks, but apart from old Tranquillo and Giacomo he no longer had any allies, he had grown bitter and spent most of his time drinking and smoking herbs he had acquired from the Indians and eventually he was expelled for violating the Charter and ignoring the censure and not attending the moments of gathering and saying that when he saw us sitting in a circle it looked like some kind of new religion and the only part of religion that appealed to him was the *gin*. Umberto said in reply that he was in favor of unplanned intercourse, but the moments of gathering awaken the higher emotions in man and that too is part of life. I think it's good that Decio left, because he was eroding the optimism born of the sap from the tree which we intend to plant here, serving as an example to the others who come after us. We live in difficult conditions, but we are joined by a brotherly bond. The interests of each correspond to the interests of the whole. First the essential, then the useful, and only after that the pleasant. Work, even if not always fun, valorizes each of us, and we reap only what we sow. Let each work according to his abilities.

OCTOBER 1855

October 15th. I'm not entirely sure whether today is October 15th. My mother was born on this day. I stopped writing a diary when we reached the settlement. I don't know where to begin, to tell the truth. She was born in Casalvieri, near Rome. A few weeks ago I had a dream that she was dead. She was lying on a bed in a black dress with her hands clasped, there were candles burning and three old ladies I didn't recognize sitting around her on chairs. I was standing at her bedside when all of a sudden she opened her eyes and put her finger to her lips. Then she stood up and beckoned to me to follow her. The weepers sat in their chairs whispering to one another and didn't notice a thing. My mother walked out of the building, I wanted to join her, but she was always six or seven steps ahead, even when I went faster to try and keep up with her. Then we came to a cemetery, my mother stopped, and I approached her but I couldn't touch her. My mother pointed to a grave and said, Here is where I live now and then she pointed to another and said, Here is where you live, now we'll be able to see each other more often. I tried to take her hand but to no avail. Then she began slowly to sink into the earth, but she didn't seem frightened, or even surprised, she looked at me seriously, perhaps even a little sternly, as she vanished into the earth, and when all that was still peeking out was her head, she closed her eyes and vanished completely. This is our sixth month here now. Decio came back to the settlement with an axe and tried to chop down the flagpole in the courtyard with the red-and-black flag flying from it. He had a dozen former settlers and a few Indians with him, one of them kept grinning and waving his machete. Almost all of them were drunk.

PATRIK OUŘEDNÍK was born in Prague, but moved to France in 1984, where he still lives. He is the author of twelve books, including fiction, essays, and poems. He is also the Czech translator of novels, short stories, and plays from such writers as François Rabelais, Alfred Jarry, Raymond Queneau, Samuel Beckett, and Boris Vian. He has received a number of prizes for his writing, including the Czech Literary Fund Award.

ALEX ZUCKER won the 2010 National Translation Award for *All This Belongs to Me*, by Petra Hůlová. *City Sister Silver*, his translation of Jáchym Topol's first novel, was selected for inclusion in *1001 Books You Must Read Before You Die*.

PETROS ABATZOGLOU, *What Does Mrs. Freeman Want?*
MICHAL AJVAZ, *The Golden Age.*
The Other City.
PIERRE ALBERT-BIROT, *Grabinoulor.*
YUZ ALESHKOVSKY, *Kangaroo.*
FELIPE ALFAU, *Chromos.*
Locos.
IVAN ÂNGELO, *The Celebration.*
The Tower of Glass.
DAVID ANTIN, *Talking.*
ANTÓNIO LOBO ANTUNES, *Knowledge of Hell.*
ALAIN ARIAS-MISSON, *Theatre of Incest.*
IFTIKHAR ARIF AND WAQAS KHWAJA, EDS., *Modern Poetry of Pakistan.*
JOHN ASHBERY AND JAMES SCHUYLER, *A Nest of Ninnies.*
GABRIELA AVIGUR-ROTEM, *Heatwave and Crazy Birds.*
HEIMRAD BÄCKER, *transcript.*
DJUNA BARNES, *Ladies Almanack.*
Ryder.
JOHN BARTH, *LETTERS.*
Sabbatical.
DONALD BARTHELME, *The King.*
Paradise.
SVETISLAV BASARA, *Chinese Letter.*
RENÉ BELLETTO, *Dying.*
MARK BINELLI, *Sacco and Vanzetti Must Die!*
ANDREI BITOV, *Pushkin House.*
ANDREJ BLATNIK, *You Do Understand.*
LOUIS PAUL BOON, *Chapel Road.*
My Little War.
Summer in Termuren.
ROGER BOYLAN, *Killoyle.*
IGNÁCIO DE LOYOLA BRANDÃO, *Anonymous Celebrity.*
The Good-Bye Angel.
Teeth under the Sun.
Zero.
BONNIE BREMSER, *Troia: Mexican Memoirs.*
CHRISTINE BROOKE-ROSE, *Amalgamemnon.*
BRIGID BROPHY, *In Transit.*
MEREDITH BROSNAN, *Mr. Dynamite.*
GERALD L. BRUNS, *Modern Poetry and the Idea of Language.*
EVGENY BUNIMOVICH AND J. KATES, EDS., *Contemporary Russian Poetry: An Anthology.*
GABRIELLE BURTON, *Heartbreak Hotel.*
MICHEL BUTOR, *Degrees.*
Mobile.
Portrait of the Artist as a Young Ape.
G. CABRERA INFANTE, *Infante's Inferno.*
Three Trapped Tigers.
JULIETA CAMPOS, *The Fear of Losing Eurydice.*
ANNE CARSON, *Eros the Bittersweet.*
ORLY CASTEL-BLOOM, *Dolly City.*
CAMILO JOSÉ CELA, *Christ versus Arizona.*
The Family of Pascual Duarte.
The Hive.
LOUIS-FERDINAND CÉLINE, *Castle to Castle.*
Conversations with Professor Y.
London Bridge.
Normance.
North.
Rigadoon.
HUGO CHARTERIS, *The Tide Is Right.*
JEROME CHARYN, *The Tar Baby.*
ERIC CHEVILLARD, *Demolishing Nisard.*
MARC CHOLODENKO, *Mordechai Schamz.*
JOSHUA COHEN, *Witz.*
EMILY HOLMES COLEMAN, *The Shutter of Snow.*
ROBERT COOVER, *A Night at the Movies.*
STANLEY CRAWFORD, *Log of the S.S. The Mrs Unguentine.*
Some Instructions to My Wife.
ROBERT CREELEY, *Collected Prose.*
RENÉ CREVEL, *Putting My Foot in It.*
RALPH CUSACK, *Cadenza.*
SUSAN DAITCH, *L.C.*
Storytown.
NICHOLAS DELBANCO, *The Count of Concord.*
Sherbrookes.
NIGEL DENNIS, *Cards of Identity.*
PETER DIMOCK, *A Short Rhetoric for Leaving the Family.*
ARIEL DORFMAN, *Konfidenz.*
COLEMAN DOWELL, *The Houses of Children.*
Island People.
Too Much Flesh and Jabez.
ARKADII DRAGOMOSHCHENKO, *Dust.*
RIKKI DUCORNET, *The Complete Butcher's Tales.*
The Fountains of Neptune.
The Jade Cabinet.
The One Marvelous Thing.
Phosphor in Dreamland.
The Stain.
The Word "Desire."
WILLIAM EASTLAKE, *The Bamboo Bed.*
Castle Keep.
Lyric of the Circle Heart.
JEAN ECHENOZ, *Chopin's Move.*
STANLEY ELKIN, *A Bad Man.*
Boswell: A Modern Comedy.
Criers and Kibitzers, Kibitzers and Criers.
The Dick Gibson Show.
The Franchiser.
George Mills.
The Living End.
The MacGuffin.
The Magic Kingdom.
Mrs. Ted Bliss.
The Rabbi of Lud.
Van Gogh's Room at Arles.
ANNIE ERNAUX, *Cleaned Out.*
LAUREN FAIRBANKS, *Muzzle Thyself.*
Sister Carrie.
LESLIE A. FIEDLER, *Love and Death in the American Novel.*
JUAN FILLOY, *Op Oloop.*
GUSTAVE FLAUBERT, *Bouvard and Pécuchet.*
KASS FLEISHER, *Talking out of School.*
FORD MADOX FORD, *The March of Literature.*
JON FOSSE, *Aliss at the Fire.*
Melancholy.
MAX FRISCH, *I'm Not Stiller.*
Man in the Holocene.

CARLOS FUENTES, *Christopher Unborn.*
  Distant Relations.
  Terra Nostra.
  Where the Air Is Clear.
JANICE GALLOWAY, *Foreign Parts.*
  The Trick Is to Keep Breathing.
WILLIAM H. GASS, *Cartesian Sonata*
  and Other Novellas.
  Finding a Form.
  A Temple of Texts.
  The Tunnel.
  Willie Masters' Lonesome Wife.
GÉRARD GAVARRY, *Hoppla! 1 2 3.*
  Making a Novel.
ETIENNE GILSON,
  The Arts of the Beautiful.
  Forms and Substances in the Arts.
C. S. GISCOMBE, *Giscome Road.*
  Here.
  Prairie Style.
DOUGLAS GLOVER, *Bad News of the Heart.*
  The Enamoured Knight.
WITOLD GOMBROWICZ,
  A Kind of Testament.
KAREN ELIZABETH GORDON,
  The Red Shoes.
GEORGI GOSPODINOV, *Natural Novel.*
JUAN GOYTISOLO, *Count Julian.*
  Exiled from Almost Everywhere.
  Juan the Landless.
  Makbara.
  Marks of Identity.
PATRICK GRAINVILLE, *The Cave of Heaven.*
HENRY GREEN, *Back.*
  Blindness.
  Concluding.
  Doting.
  Nothing.
JIŘÍ GRUŠA, *The Questionnaire.*
GABRIEL GUDDING,
  Rhode Island Notebook.
MELA HARTWIG, *Am I a Redundant*
  Human Being?
JOHN HAWKES, *The Passion Artist.*
  Whistlejacket.
ALEKSANDAR HEMON, ED.,
  Best European Fiction.
AIDAN HIGGINS, *A Bestiary.*
  Balcony of Europe.
  Bornholm Night-Ferry.
  Darkling Plain: Texts for the Air.
  Flotsam and Jetsam.
  Langrishe, Go Down.
  Scenes from a Receding Past.
  Windy Arbours.
KEIZO HINO, *Isle of Dreams.*
KAZUSHI HOSAKA, *Plainsong.*
ALDOUS HUXLEY, *Antic Hay.*
  Crome Yellow.
  Point Counter Point.
  Those Barren Leaves.
  Time Must Have a Stop.
NAOYUKI II, *The Shadow of a Blue Cat.*
MIKHAIL IOSSEL AND JEFF PARKER, EDS.,
  Amerika: Russian Writers View the
  United States.
GERT JONKE, *The Distant Sound.*
  Geometric Regional Novel.
  Homage to Czerny.
  The System of Vienna.

JACQUES JOUET, *Mountain R.*
  Savage.
  Upstaged.
CHARLES JULIET, *Conversations with*
  Samuel Beckett and Bram van
  Velde.
MIEKO KANAI, *The Word Book.*
YORAM KANIUK, *Life on Sandpaper.*
HUGH KENNER, *The Counterfeiters.*
  Flaubert, Joyce and Beckett:
  The Stoic Comedians.
  Joyce's Voices.
DANILO KIŠ, *Garden, Ashes.*
  A Tomb for Boris Davidovich.
ANITA KONKKA, *A Fool's Paradise.*
GEORGE KONRÁD, *The City Builder.*
TADEUSZ KONWICKI, *A Minor Apocalypse.*
  The Polish Complex.
MENIS KOUMANDAREAS, *Koula.*
ELAINE KRAF, *The Princess of 72nd Street.*
JIM KRUSOE, *Iceland.*
EWA KURYLUK, *Century 21.*
EMILIO LASCANO TEGUI, *On Elegance*
  While Sleeping.
ERIC LAURRENT, *Do Not Touch.*
HERVÉ LE TELLIER, *The Sextine Chapel.*
  A Thousand Pearls (for a Thousand
  Pennies)
VIOLETTE LEDUC, *La Bâtarde.*
EDOUARD LEVÉ, *Suicide.*
SUZANNE JILL LEVINE, *The Subversive*
  Scribe: Translating Latin
  American Fiction.
DEBORAH LEVY, *Billy and Girl.*
  Pillow Talk in Europe and Other
  Places.
JOSÉ LEZAMA LIMA, *Paradiso.*
ROSA LIKSOM, *Dark Paradise.*
OSMAN LINS, *Avalovara.*
  The Queen of the Prisons of Greece.
ALF MAC LOCHLAINN,
  The Corpus in the Library.
  Out of Focus.
RON LOEWINSOHN, *Magnetic Field(s).*
MINA LOY, *Stories and Essays of Mina Loy.*
BRIAN LYNCH, *The Winner of Sorrow.*
D. KEITH MANO, *Take Five.*
MICHELINE AHARONIAN MARCOM,
  The Mirror in the Well.
BEN MARCUS,
  The Age of Wire and String.
WALLACE MARKFIELD,
  Teitlebaum's Window.
  To an Early Grave.
DAVID MARKSON, *Reader's Block.*
  Springer's Progress.
  Wittgenstein's Mistress.
CAROLE MASO, *AVA.*
LADISLAV MATEJKA AND KRYSTYNA
  POMORSKA, EDS.,
  Readings in Russian Poetics:
  Formalist and Structuralist Views.
HARRY MATHEWS,
  The Case of the Persevering Maltese:
  Collected Essays.
  Cigarettes.
  The Conversions.
  The Human Country: New and
  Collected Stories.
  The Journalist.

SELECTED DALKEY ARCHIVE PAPERBACKS

My Life in CIA.
Singular Pleasures.
The Sinking of the Odradek
    Stadium.
Tlooth.
20 Lines a Day.
JOSEPH MCELROY,
    Night Soul and Other Stories.
THOMAS MCGONIGLE,
    Going to Patchogue.
ROBERT L. MCLAUGHLIN, ED., *Innovations:*
    An Anthology of
    Modern & Contemporary Fiction.
ABDELWAHAB MEDDEB, *Talismano.*
HERMAN MELVILLE, *The Confidence-Man.*
AMANDA MICHALOPOULOU, *I'd Like.*
STEVEN MILLHAUSER,
    The Barnum Museum.
    In the Penny Arcade.
RALPH J. MILLS, JR.,
    Essays on Poetry.
MOMUS, *The Book of Jokes.*
CHRISTINE MONTALBETTI, *Western.*
OLIVE MOORE, *Spleen.*
NICHOLAS MOSLEY, *Accident.*
    Assassins.
    Catastrophe Practice.
    Children of Darkness and Light.
    Experience and Religion.
    God's Hazard.
    The Hesperides Tree.
    Hopeful Monsters.
    Imago Bird.
    Impossible Object.
    Inventing God.
    Judith.
    Look at the Dark.
    Natalie Natalia.
    Paradoxes of Peace.
    Serpent.
    Time at War.
    The Uses of Slime Mould:
        Essays of Four Decades.
WARREN MOTTE,
    Fables of the Novel: French Fiction
        since 1990.
    Fiction Now: The French Novel in
        the 21st Century.
    Oulipo: A Primer of Potential
        Literature.
YVES NAVARRE, *Our Share of Time.*
    Sweet Tooth.
DOROTHY NELSON, *In Night's City.*
    Tar and Feathers.
ESHKOL NEVO, *Homesick.*
WILFRIDO D. NOLLEDO, *But for the Lovers.*
FLANN O'BRIEN,
    At Swim-Two-Birds.
    At War.
    The Best of Myles.
    The Dalkey Archive.
    Further Cuttings.
    The Hard Life.
    The Poor Mouth.
    The Third Policeman.
CLAUDE OLLIER, *The Mise-en-Scène.*
    Wert and the Life Without End.
PATRIK OUŘEDNÍK, *Europeana.*
    The Opportune Moment, 1855.
BORIS PAHOR, *Necropolis.*

FERNANDO DEL PASO,
    News from the Empire.
    Palinuro of Mexico.
ROBERT PINGET, *The Inquisitory.*
    Mahu or The Material.
    Trio.
MANUEL PUIG,
    Betrayed by Rita Hayworth.
    The Buenos Aires Affair.
    Heartbreak Tango.
RAYMOND QUENEAU, *The Last Days.*
    Odile.
    Pierrot Mon Ami.
    Saint Glinglin.
ANN QUIN, *Berg.*
    Passages.
    Three.
    Tripticks.
ISHMAEL REED,
    The Free-Lance Pallbearers.
    The Last Days of Louisiana Red.
    Ishmael Reed: The Plays.
    Juice!
    Reckless Eyeballing.
    The Terrible Threes.
    The Terrible Twos.
    Yellow Back Radio Broke-Down.
JOÃO UBALDO RIBEIRO, *House of the*
    Fortunate Buddhas.
JEAN RICARDOU, *Place Names.*
RAINER MARIA RILKE, *The Notebooks of*
    Malte Laurids Brigge.
JULIÁN RÍOS, *The House of Ulysses.*
    Larva: A Midsummer Night's Babel.
    Poundemonium.
    Procession of Shadows.
AUGUSTO ROA BASTOS, *I the Supreme.*
DANIËL ROBBERECHTS,
    Arriving in Avignon.
JEAN ROLIN, *The Explosion of the*
    Radiator Hose.
OLIVIER ROLIN, *Hotel Crystal.*
ALIX CLEO ROUBAUD, *Alix's Journal.*
JACQUES ROUBAUD, *The Form of a*
    City Changes Faster, Alas, Than
    the Human Heart.
    The Great Fire of London.
    Hortense in Exile.
    Hortense Is Abducted.
    The Loop.
    The Plurality of Worlds of Lewis.
    The Princess Hoppy.
    Some Thing Black.
LEON S. ROUDIEZ, *French Fiction Revisited.*
RAYMOND ROUSSEL, *Impressions of Africa.*
VEDRANA RUDAN, *Night.*
STIG SÆTERBAKKEN, *Siamese.*
LYDIE SALVAYRE, *The Company of Ghosts.*
    Everyday Life.
    The Lecture.
    Portrait of the Writer as a
        Domesticated Animal.
    The Power of Flies.
LUIS RAFAEL SÁNCHEZ,
    Macho Camacho's Beat.
SEVERO SARDUY, *Cobra & Maitreya.*
NATHALIE SARRAUTE,
    Do You Hear Them?
    Martereau.
    The Planetarium.

FOR A FULL LIST OF PUBLICATIONS, VISIT:

SELECTED DALKEY ARCHIVE PAPERBACKS

ARNO SCHMIDT, *Collected Novellas.*
Collected Stories.
Nobodaddy's Children.
Two Novels.
ASAF SCHURR, *Motti.*
CHRISTINE SCHUTT, *Nightwork.*
GAIL SCOTT, *My Paris.*
DAMION SEARLS, *What We Were Doing
and Where We Were Going.*
JUNE AKERS SEESE,
Is This What Other Women Feel Too?
What Waiting Really Means.
BERNARD SHARE, *Inish.*
Transit.
AURELIE SHEEHAN,
Jack Kerouac Is Pregnant.
VIKTOR SHKLOVSKY, *Bowstring.*
Knight's Move.
*A Sentimental Journey:
Memoirs 1917–1922.*
Energy of Delusion: A Book on Plot.
Literature and Cinematography.
Theory of Prose.
Third Factory.
Zoo, or Letters Not about Love.
CLAUDE SIMON, *The Invitation.*
PIERRE SINIAC, *The Collaborators.*
JOSEF ŠKVORECKÝ, *The Engineer of
Human Souls.*
GILBERT SORRENTINO,
Aberration of Starlight.
Blue Pastoral.
Crystal Vision.
*Imaginative Qualities of Actual
Things.*
Mulligan Stew.
Pack of Lies.
Red the Fiend.
The Sky Changes.
Something Said.
Splendide-Hôtel.
Steelwork.
Under the Shadow.
W. M. SPACKMAN,
The Complete Fiction.
ANDRZEJ STASIUK, *Fado.*
GERTRUDE STEIN,
Lucy Church Amiably.
The Making of Americans.
A Novel of Thank You.
LARS SVENDSEN, *A Philosophy of Evil.*
PIOTR SZEWC, *Annihilation.*
GONÇALO M. TAVARES, *Jerusalem.*
*Learning to Pray in the Age of
Technology.*
LUCIAN DAN TEODOROVICI,
Our Circus Presents . . .
STEFAN THEMERSON, *Hobson's Island.*
The Mystery of the Sardine.
Tom Harris.
JOHN TOOMEY, *Sleepwalker.*
JEAN-PHILIPPE TOUSSAINT,
The Bathroom.
Camera.
Monsieur.
Running Away.
Self-Portrait Abroad.
Television.
DUMITRU TSEPENEAG,
Hotel Europa.

The Necessary Marriage.
Pigeon Post.
Vain Art of the Fugue.
ESTHER TUSQUETS, *Stranded.*
DUBRAVKA UGRESIC,
Lend Me Your Character.
Thank You for Not Reading.
MATI UNT, *Brecht at Night.*
Diary of a Blood Donor.
Things in the Night.
ÁLVARO URIBE AND OLIVIA SEARS, EDS.,
*Best of Contemporary Mexican
Fiction.*
ELOY URROZ, *Friction.*
The Obstacles.
LUISA VALENZUELA, *Dark Desires and
the Others.*
He Who Searches.
MARJA-LIISA VARTIO,
The Parson's Widow.
PAUL VERHAEGHEN, *Omega Minor.*
BORIS VIAN, *Heartsnatcher.*
LLORENÇ VILLALONGA, *The Dolls' Room.*
ORNELA VORPSI, *The Country Where No
One Ever Dies.*
AUSTRYN WAINHOUSE, *Hedyphagetica.*
PAUL WEST,
Words for a Deaf Daughter & Gala.
CURTIS WHITE,
America's Magic Mountain.
The Idea of Home.
Memories of My Father Watching TV.
*Monstrous Possibility: An Invitation
to Literary Politics.*
Requiem.
DIANE WILLIAMS, *Excitability:
Selected Stories.*
Romancer Erector.
DOUGLAS WOOLF, *Wall to Wall.*
Ya! & John-Juan.
JAY WRIGHT, *Polynomials and Pollen.*
*The Presentable Art of Reading
Absence.*
PHILIP WYLIE, *Generation of Vipers.*
MARGUERITE YOUNG, *Angel in the Forest.*
Miss MacIntosh, My Darling.
REYOUNG, *Unbabbling.*
VLADO ŽABOT, *The Succubus.*
ZORAN ŽIVKOVIĆ, *Hidden Camera.*
LOUIS ZUKOFSKY, *Collected Fiction.*
SCOTT ZWIREN, *God Head.*